PER VERSE
VENGEANCE

PER VERSE
VENGEANCE

JOSEPH SCIUTO

IGUANA

Published by Iguana Books
720 Bathurst Street, Suite 303
Toronto, Ontario, Canada
M5S 2R4

ISBN (paperback): 978-1-77180-291-8
ISBN (EPUB): 978-1-77180-292-5
ISBN (Kindle): 978-1-77180-273-2

Editor: Paula Chiarcos
Cover image: Photo by Tomo Nogi on Unsplash
Cover design: Daniella Postavsky

This is an original print edition of *Per Verse Vengeance.*

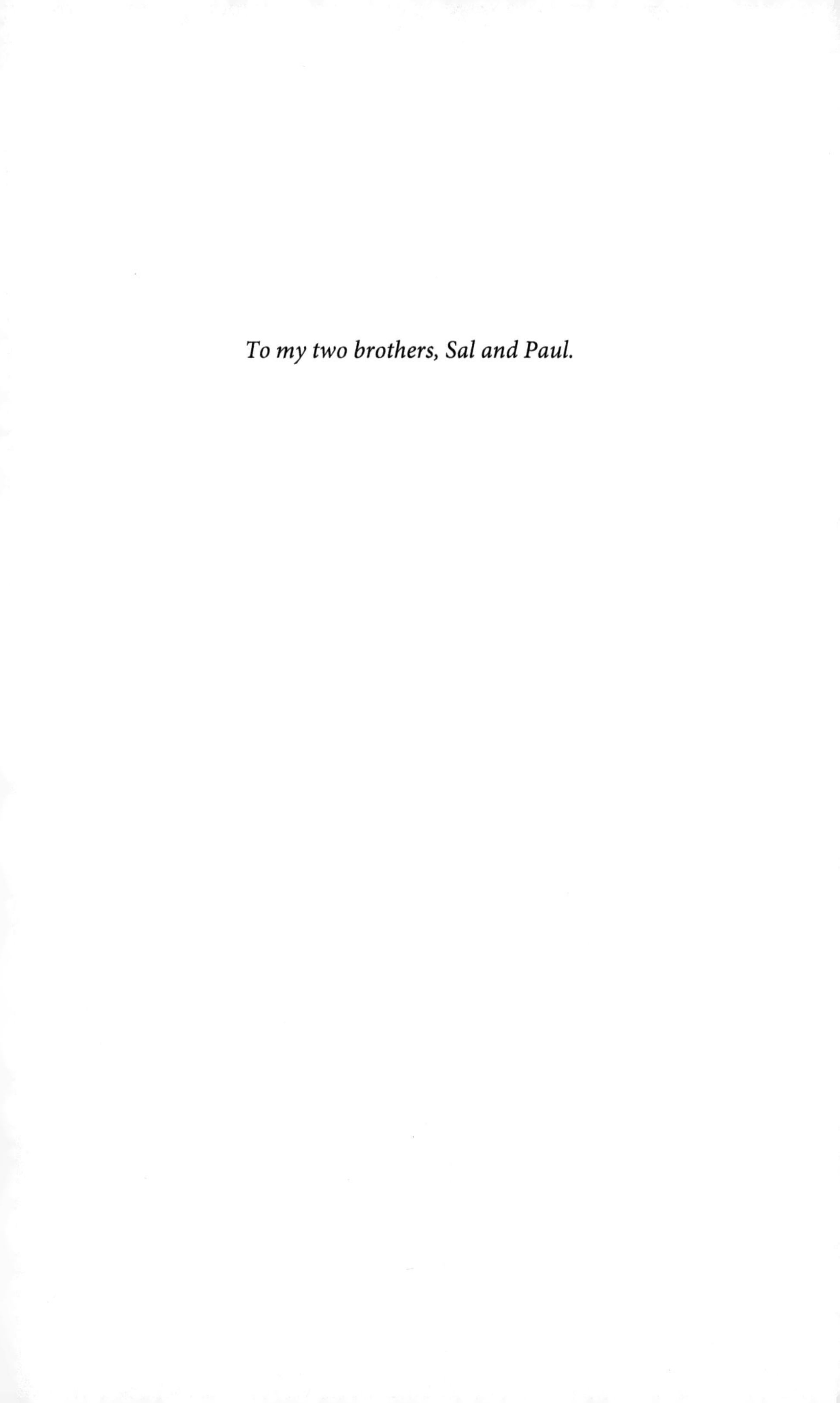

To my two brothers, Sal and Paul.

One

Nicholas Righetti looks like a movie star. His demeanor, in sharp contrast, is easy, unpretentious and accommodating. He is clean-shaven with a square jaw, dark brown eyes and wavy black hair that falls forward against his olive skin. He leans lightly against the crowded bar as his eyes dot across the casino floor at the fabulous Venetian Hotel in Las Vegas where Frank Sinatra's "Lady Luck" vibrates in the air around him. His eyes suddenly become transfixed on the beautiful woman walking toward him.

Schooled and polished, Nicole Tyler would make a tantalizing politician — the first in line to pull the switch on a deserving death-row inmate and then, without any qualm of conscience, she'd go out and enjoy a fine bottle of wine and a delicious meal. She is steadfast in her opinions and has a well-founded mistrust of everything, especially men. Her long dark hair, cut perfectly around her lovely face, bounces up and down in perfect harmony with every measured step she takes. She wears an expensive two-piece white suit that one would expect to find on a well-placed business executive. Her emerald eyes are hypnotic and once transfixed on a certain object they seem to linger on that object long after she has left the room. She is calculating, exceptionally intelligent and more than capable of taking care of herself in the most difficult of situations.

She slides past the crowd and stops before the only empty chair at the bar, where Nick is standing.

"Is this chair taken?"

"No."

"You sure? You seem a little uncertain."

Nick laughs and pulls the chair out for her. "It's all yours."

She sits down. "Thank you. This is my favorite bar in this whole disgusting town. It's the only one where you can ask the bartender for a mojito and not get a dirty look."

"You don't strike me as one who is easily intimidated, especially not by a bartender."

"I'm not." She leans forward as she brushes her long dark hair off her shoulder and orders her drink. She continues, "Just passing through?"

"On my way to Los Angeles."

"Me too. Lose much?"

"Not much … certainly not my pants and shirt … maybe a sock or two," Nick remarks as the bartender puts a mojito down in front of them.

Nicole takes a long sip and smiles. "Simply wonderful. Don't forget to tip the bartender when you offer to pick up my tab."

"You're pretty sure of yourself."

"Would you like a taste?" Nicole asks as she flirtatiously offers her glass to Nick.

"Thanks, but I'll stick with beer."

"I'm not contagious."

"Sure you are."

"Maybe … but only in a good way."

"I guess that depends on your definition."

"Do you live in Los Angeles?" Nicole asks, glancing up from her drink.

"I wouldn't call it my residence, but I pass through quite a bit visiting family. And you, what's your reason for going there?"

"It's simply the first stop on my farewell tour."

"Leaving Vegas for good?"

"Yes, for good!"

"Business off?" Nick asks.

"Seriously, do I look like I'm suffering?"

"That depends," Nick replies.

"On what?"

"The view."

"Well, this is the best view you'll ever get of me."

"I doubt that," Nick comments as he motions to the bartender to refill their drinks.

"Two is my limit. Don't want to dig too deep into your pockets."

"So, where is your final destination?" Nick asks.

"Somewhere I can be invisible."

"Like … witness protection?"

"I don't think I qualify. At least, not yet."

The bartender places their new drinks down. Nicole, once again, offers Nick a taste. "This time you don't have to worry. My lips haven't touched the glass."

"It's not your lips that I'm worried about. I simply don't like to mix."

"Scared to get your tippy-toes wet?"

"Maybe."

"You don't seem like the type to get easily frightened," Nicole remarks as she takes a sip from her drink.

"You don't know me, and if this is the best the view gets, you never will."

"Don't expect me to shed any tears."

"Wouldn't dream of it," Nick remarks.

"Flying back to Los Angeles?" Nicole asks.

"No! I'm hitching a ride with you."

"Cute … real cute. And what in the world makes you think I'm taking on passengers?"

"I'll pay for the gas and drinks."

"Sweet, but you're going to have to do a lot better than that."

"It's a long ride," Nick remarks.

"I drive fast."

"Not fast enough to hide from whatever you're running from."

"And what makes you think I'm running from anything?"

"Why else would you want to remain invisible?"

"Tired of prying eyes like yours undressing me."

"That's the second mojito talking."

"I've barely touched it."

"Yeah, but I could smell the bourbon on your breath the second you sat down."

"You must be smelling someone else. This is a bar, after all."

"No one is drinking bourbon."

"Wow! Very observant … is that a natural gift or did you have to train yourself?"

"A little of both."

Nick reaches for his beer, obviously favoring his right side. One could easily imagine a lingering football injury.

"You survived some tough shit?" Nicole asks.

"Probably no tougher shit than you."

"Do you have a profession?"

"Not at the moment. Any suggestions?"

"Why not train to be an astronaut?" Nicole suggests.

"But that would mean months and years away from you," Nick replies.

"Don't worry, I can handle it. Remember … I'm the one who wants to be invisible."

"But not invisible from me…"

"And why not you? What makes you so special?"

"I'm not easily intimidated," Nick replies as Nicole looks directly into his dark eyes.

"Is that so."

"And I try not to make harsh judgments without knowing all the facts."

"And yet … you've had no problem profiling me since you saw me across the room."

"What can I say … you're special."

"Before and after?"

"Why would there be a difference?"

"Because there usually is," Nicole replies.

"I can change that."

"It's too late. I'm retired."

"And how's that working out?"

"It's only been a day … but a long time in the making. All that's left is the paperwork."

"And a lot of loose ends."

"Yes, but not for long."

"You're not one to forget?" Nick asks.

"Nor do I forgive."

"That's a tough maxim to live by."

"I wasn't given much of a choice."

"Maybe you should look to a Higher Power?"

"That boat sailed years ago … a lot of requests and no responses. But please, feel free to say all the prayers you want for me."

"I'll put you on the list, but first I need a name."

"How about … beautiful girl you met at the bar, who drank the drinks you bought her and then told you to take a hike."

"You need to do a little better than that. After all, my time is precious."

She stretches her hand toward him. "Nicole … how is that?" she asks as she shakes his hand.

"Nice. But did you just make that up?"

"Maybe, but since I doubt you'll have any better luck than me, it should do … for now at least."

She places her empty glass on the bar. "That's my limit. Time to go pack. Would you like to help me lift some dead weight? I promise, there's a beer in it for you."

Nick pays the bill and follows Nicole to the elevator. "You didn't forget to leave a good tip?"

"I've never left a bad tip in my life," Nick remarks as Nicole stops and looks directly at him, smiling softly. "Nice! Very nice!"

"I didn't realize you were staying at this hotel."

"Just for the day. My lease expired yesterday and I still had a little unfinished business to take care of," Nicole replies as they get into the elevator. "And your name?"

"Nick."

"Sweet," Nicole remarks as they get off the elevator and walk toward her room.

When they enter the hotel room, she goes straight to the bathroom while he looks around, then stops. He squints through a crack between the closet doors then pulls them open … and sees a bald, overweight, naked man tied to a chair, with a bullet hole through his head. Nick stares at the corpse for a long moment. The dead man stares back at him. "You have a dead man in your closet."

The toilet flushes and the door to the bathroom opens. "Did you say something? I couldn't hear."

Nick walks toward the bathroom and for a moment, watches Nicole fixing her hair and makeup in the mirror.

"You have a dead man in your closet."

"My God! You really are observant."

She applies a finishing touch of lipstick and turns toward him. "And if you don't help me get rid of him real soon he's going to start stinking up the room."

In a few quick strides, he's behind her and he grabs her by the arm and turns her around. "Don't act cute with me."

"Get your hand off of me."

Nick lets go. "I could call the police."

"Maybe if you knew what this son of a bitch has done to me and dozens of other girls, you might think differently."

"I don't need to get involved in this."

"You have a sister?"

"I don't see what that has to do with anything."

"Well, if you loved that sister and she was unfortunate enough to be one of the dozens of women under his control, you would've been the one who put the bullet through his head."

For a moment, Nick sees the pain and suffering in her emerald eyes. He looks back down at the body and across at her. She sighs deeply, closes her eyes and shakes her head. "I guess you don't have a sister. At least, not one that you love." She steps around him and walks to the body. She reaches into her pocket for a switchblade and snaps it open. "So are you going to help or are you just going to stand there and look at me?"

Nick hesitates, but then his feet start moving and as she cuts through the tape and rope holding the body to the chair, he is there to steady the corpse as it falls forward.

Nicole points to a luggage cart. "We can wheel him down to the service elevator."

"Is that your plan? There have to be cameras all over this place."

"The cameras on this floor have all been deactivated."

"Of course they have. Should I even ask who this guy is?"

"Why don't you leave the questions for later ... on our way to Los Angeles? All you need to know is that the disgusting pig got exactly what he deserved."

They struggle with the corpse but finally manage to lift him onto the cart. Then Nicole walks to the door. "Wait here. I'll be back in a minute."

She looks both ways down the hotel hallway, steps out of the room, gently closes the door and walks about a hundred feet to the service elevator. She presses the up button and waits, her eyes scanning the empty hallway like a pair of searchlights. The elevator grows louder as it moves between the floors. When it stops and the doors slide open, Nicole smiles at the empty compartment. She takes off her strappy, three-inch Manolo Blahnik sandals and drops them on the edge of the elevator door, then scuttles back across the carpeted hallway to the room where Nick holds the handle of the cart.

"Let's go."

Nick rolls the cart toward the door as Nicole, once again, checks the hallway. He pushes the cart out and follows her to the elevator. She's already busy taking her shoes out from between the doors, then she pushes them wide open. Nick rolls the cart into the elevator and steps out and Nicole reaches in and playfully runs her hand across every button to every floor in the hotel. The elevator doors close as Nick and Nicole walk back toward the room.

"I'm surprised. No final words for the deceased," Nick comments.

"I said my final words just before the bastard departed this world."

They re-enter the room and Nicole opens the door to the minibar and hands Nick a beer. She drops a piece of ice into a glass and coats it with bourbon, then sits on the bed. She crosses her legs as she admires her perfectly manicured hands.

"Now that wasn't so hard, was it?"

"I thought two was your limit," Nick remarks.

"Two *mojitos*."

She finishes off the bourbon and looks down at her watch. "Time to go."

She gets up, zips up her one piece of luggage, grabs the handle and starts toward the door.

"Wait a second." Nick takes out his phone. She turns around and before she can get a hand up to block her face, he takes a picture.

"What the hell is that for?"

He takes another. "Insurance! Even though, I doubt you could walk through any crowded building without at least a hundred guys remembering you."

"Cute … now why don't you delete them like a nice little boy?"

"I don't think so," Nick replies. "I'm staying at a different hotel. Give me an hour and I'll meet you behind this one. What are you driving?"

"A black Jag. Don't be late," Nicole warns him, turning to the door. "Patience," he says, following her. Then he opens the door for her and watches as she walks down the hallway.

Nick enters his hotel room, flicks on the light and walks to the window on the far side. The heavy drapes are open and for a long moment, he stares out at the lights of Las Vegas. Then he turns and walks to his suitcase that lies on the bed, opens it and reaches under his clothes. The .38-caliber revolver is cool as he slips it out, then reaches in again for its holster. He attaches the holster to the back of his belt, then places the gun into it and looks into a mirror to make sure that his sports coat conceals the weapon. He turns the light off and walks out of the room.

Two

Through the driver's side mirror of her black Jaguar, Nicole sees Nick walking toward her. She watches him like an appraiser inspecting a piece of art, then gently presses down on the button to unlock the passenger door. Nick tosses his luggage onto the backseat then pulls open the front door and sits down next to her.

"Right on time," Nicole remarks.

"Think I wouldn't show?"

"I was hoping you wouldn't."

"That's not very nice."

"I told you, I don't play nice."

"Well, you better start."

"What's that suppose to mean?"

"If you really want to be invisible, it's a lot easier if you stop playing the mean girl all the time."

"And how would you know?"

"Experience, sweetheart."

Nicole slides it into drive and they head down the Vegas Strip.

"How long have you lived here?" Nick asks.

"Seven years."

"No final words before leaving this desert paradise … for what I presume is your last time?"

"No."

"No friends you're going to miss?"

"What do you think?"

"Stupid question."

A traffic light turns red and Nicole slams on the brakes, sending Nick's luggage in the backseat flying. "Sorry about that. The lights in Vegas have never been in sync. You think I'd be used to it by now."

When Nick turns to rearrange his luggage, she glances at his backside, where his holstered gun is sticking out from behind his sports coat, and sighs.

The light turns green and she continues down the Strip. "So do *you* have many friends here in Vegas?"

"Not a one. Just business associates."

"And what type of business are we talking about?"

"Nothing you'd be interested in ... that is, if you're serious about staying invisible."

Nicole turns off the Vegas Strip and onto Highway 15 toward Los Angeles. She drives about fifteen miles, past the new construction sites and communities springing up all around Vegas, and then hammers the brakes and veers off the road at a desolate, dimly lit stretch of the highway with the desert on both sides.

"I think my back tire might be low. I'll be right back." She gets out of the car and walks around the back as Nick keeps an eye on her in the rearview mirror. She opens the trunk and blocks Nick's view. She pulls out a small-caliber pistol from inside the trunk, then slips toward the passenger door and puts the gun against the back of Nick's head.

"Get out. Slowly."

"What are you doing?" Nick asks, but he gets out of the car.

"Now take your gun out and put it on the seat ... and your phone."

"You're making a big mistake here," Nick remarks, but he does as she says.

She shoves him away from the car toward the surrounding desert, hard enough that he falls to his knees, a few feet away from her. She keeps the gun pointed at his head. "How much did they pay you?"

"I don't know what you're talking about."

The road curves out of sight. A dry desert wind blows, accompanied by the skittish sound of lizards and a howl of a coyote in the distance. "I'll ask you one more time, how much did they pay you?" Suddenly a speeding eighteen-wheeler appears out of nowhere, and Nicole startles at the bright lights and roaring engine. Nick uses the moment to jump toward her and knock the gun out of hand. Then a swift and nasty kick to the stomach sends her flying backwards to the ground. He follows her down, grabs her arms and flings her toward a small embankment. Nicole rolls across the hard ground, gasping. She makes it onto her knees, then starts to vomit … a string of green bile now covering her expensive suit and shoes. She finally catches her breath. "Did you really have to hit me so hard?"

"Sweetheart, that's the least of your problems," Nick replies and points her gun at her.

"Go ahead … do it."

"If I were you, I wouldn't be in such a rush to die because on the off chance there is a Heaven and a Hell … I don't see Saint Peter greeting you at the Golden Gates."

"Fuck you!"

"Now, now. That type of language is not going to help your case one bit."

"What do you want?"

"I want what every boy who grows up in the Bronx wants … to play center field for the Yankees."

"Well, I can't do anything about that. But if you let me live, I can double … triple what they're paying you. Three … four hundred thousand. All the money I have."

"You sad, pathetic child. I give four hundred thousand a year to my least favorite charities. Just stay where you are while I go get you some clean clothes out of the car. Make a move and I'll shoot your knee caps and make the rest of your life really miserable."

Nick opens the trunk and looks down at an armory of weapons. "You have an arsenal back here, Nicole."

"They're all registered and licensed."

"I'm sure they are," Nick says to himself as he grabs a dress, shoes and a bottle of mouthwash from her luggage and slams the trunk shut. He flings her clothes at her as he walks past to pick up his gun and phone from the passenger seat.

Then he turns to watch as she starts to undress.

"Can't you at least show me some decency and turn around."

"Nope. The last thing I'm doing is turning my back on you. Believe me, whatever you have to offer, I've seen plenty times before."

She takes off her soiled clothes and shoes and puts on the clean stuff. Nick flips her the bottle of mouthwash and she rinses out her mouth. "Can you get me a bag for my clothes?"

"Let the vultures have them."

"This outfit cost me over two thousand dollars."

"I said leave it. Be happy it's not your little hide that the vultures are feeding on."

Nick follows her back to the car, grabs the back of her neck and forces her down into the passenger seat. Then he opens the glove compartment and takes out another pistol and remarks, "Licensed!" He walks around to the driver's side and sits down.

"I don't like other people driving my car."

"Get use to it. Your driving privileges have been revoked."

Nick pulls back onto the road as Nicole glares out the window, tapping her fingers against the glass.

"Has anyone ever told you, you drive like an old lady?" she asks.

"I would be very careful. You don't smell like a bed of roses and I'm seriously contemplating throwing you in the trunk."

"Wow. You really know how to make a lady feel good about her herself."

"You just tried to kill me, you little psychopath."

"I wasn't going to kill you. I was just going to push you and your luggage down the hill."

"Bullshit. You had every intention of killing me."

"Okay, maybe, but probably not…"

"I can only imagine the trail of mayhem and horror you must've left behind … to actually think there's a hitman after you."

"You don't know anything about me."

"I know you have no problem killing people."

"Circumstances you know nothing about."

"Well then, why don't you enlighten me? Why not start with the dead guy in your hotel room?"

Nicole turns to the window again, sighs and continues to drum her fingers. She looks forlornly out at the spectral surroundings. A canopy of stars shines down upon them as the headlights of the car pierce the dark and lonely landscape.

"He was my boss. The head of the Las Vegas chapter of high-end prostitutes, mostly from Appalachia, sold by our parents with the promise that we would enjoy a better life than we could ever have imagined. The son of a bitch always had an eye for me. But it was forbidden by the council for any member … especially bosses … to have sex with any of the girls. I made it clear to him that I was willing to take the risk and keep quiet. He couldn't resist and now he's riding up and down in a service elevator with a bullet through his head."

"So it was revenge."

"He got what he deserved."

"And this *council* … are they the money behind this operation?"

"Yeah. Wall Street types, gangsters, Hollywood producers. It's simple. Nothing sells quite like sex, and believe me, people will pay any price to live out their twisted fantasies."

"Do you know any of these council members?"

"A couple, but only by name."

"Start from the beginning."

"The beginning is a long time ago."

"I've got plenty of time. One of the benefits of driving like an old lady."

Nicole taps the side window repeatedly … her eyes dotting across scattered cacti. She can almost feel their thorny stems reaching in and stabbing her battered body and mind.

"It's better if I don't tell you any more. The less you know … the better."

Nick almost smiles, then lifts his gun and points it at her. "Start talking."

"Like you would actually shoot me."

"You know, you're not nearly as attractive right now as you were at the bar. So stop with the attitude and start talking."

"Whatever you say, tough guy. It was a dark and gloomy night, a long, long time ago and little Nicole—"

Nick shoves the barrel of his gun into her side.

"Hey, that really hurt! The next time, I swear I'll heave all over you."

The gun jams into her side again, and she jumps. "Fine, I'll tell you the whole friggin' story."

Nick settles back in his seat but keeps the gun pointed at her.

"One day, a fancy lady pulled up in front of our trailer … knocked on the door and made my parents an offer they couldn't refuse. Fifty thousand dollars for their fifteen-year-old daughter."

Nick looks at her with disbelieving eyes. "Yeah, I know it's hard to believe. Fifty thousand for a hillbilly whose only redeeming and appealing quality was her looks. I guess they'd been scouting me for some time … said they wanted me for a modeling agency. They promised my parents I would get a superb education … I'd be provided for like a princess. Naturally, my loving parents signed on the dotted line, waiving all parental rights."

Nicole laughs as she looks at the expression on Nick's face. "What? Like your parents wouldn't have done the same?"

Nick suppresses the desire to reply and she continues, "When I came home from school that day, my younger brother and baby sister were outside admiring a limousine in front of our trailer. Madam Johnson was still there. My parents told me I'd be going on a trip with her ... to an enchanted place. Just thinking about driving in a car reserved for movie stars and I had my first real orgasm. I was wet all over. It was like I peed myself."

Nick smiles faintly ... it's hard to imagine an innocent fifteen-year-old Nicole.

"I thought you might like that analogy."

"Cute ... and distasteful," Nick remarks.

"You haven't heard anything yet."

Nicole looks down at her hands, takes a breath and glances out the window again. "In the limo ... Madam Johnson sort of ... examined me ... like I was cattle or something. She ran her hands all over my face, my hair, my breasts ... even my feet and hands."

Nicole's voice trails off and without looking at her, Nick can tell she's lost in her memory. "Then she ... she put her fingers into me ... my vagina. Poked around like she was looking for some hidden treasure. I just froze. I didn't stop her. I remember she said, *Very nice.* And then just wiped her hands off on a Kleenex. We went on a private plane. There was another girl, Elizabeth. They gave us bottled water — first time in my life I had water that wasn't from a tap — and broiled fish and vegetables."

Nicole sniffs the air. "My God, I really do smell. Maybe, you *should* put me in the trunk."

"Just keep talking."

"Why? You have a time machine? It's not like we can go back and change things. I don't see the purpose in rehashing this, and don't you dare shove that gun into my side again."

Nick places the gun in his left side coat pocket as a grimace of pain streaks across his face.

"Why do you favor your right side so much?" Nicole asks. "Were you involved in an accident?"

"I guess you could call it that."

"Recent?"

"A little over a year ago. It seems to flare up whenever I have to flip a naughty little girl over my shoulder."

"Bullshit! I noticed it back at the bar. So, what happened?"

"Just an accident."

Nick turns on the radio as Nicole rests her head against the side window and studies his handsome face as she listens to Bob Seger's, "Roll Me Away." She suddenly reaches down and shuts off the radio.

"Don't like that song?" Nick asks.

"I love that song. That's the problem," Nicole replies. "Are you familiar with upstate New York?"

"A little."

"Well, that plane carrying Elizabeth and I landed on the grounds of this huge estate along the Hudson. Until this very day, after nearly a decade in Las Vegas, I've still never seen an estate that big. Makes the new Yankee stadium look like a toy. It has a hospital, cemetery, libraries, a gym bigger than Rupp Arena, dance halls, screening rooms, classrooms, auditoriums ... an unholy city hidden by an impenetrable forest and the mighty Hudson."

The darkness on both sides of them, like a cloud of discontent silently forming a commonality ... a confessional bond, is punctured only by the headlights of the car as it pierces the black solitude that lies ahead.

"At first, I thought I was living some type of dream and Elizabeth, who was my roommate the entire time we were there, thought that Jesus had delivered her to the Promised Land. Her family was very religious ... Bible-thumping hypocrites who preached the word of God but had no problem selling off their daughter. After all, they had four others. Our room was bigger than my entire home back in Kentucky and we shared our own bathroom. Our beds were huge and comfortable. The pillows smelled like flowers. There were about twenty of us girls, all about my age. And one Miss Lynch. We called her our hall monitor. We were supposed to go to her if we had any questions."

Nicole starts to laugh. "I'll never forget Elizabeth's first question to Miss Lynch. She asked if we had to pay rent to stay there. Poor Elizabeth, she was way too good for this world."

"The two of you didn't keep in touch after you left this palace?" Nick asks.

Nicole's eyes well up with tears that stream down her face like a torrential storm. She trembles and stutters as Nick reaches over and takes her hand. "No! Please don't, please don't touch me." He lets go as she desperately tries to regain control.

"Yes, we were both assigned to Vegas and we shared an apartment the entire time. At least ... until a few weeks ago when I was called down to the city morgue to identify her body. Maybe she's finally made it to the Promised Land?" She starts to choke up again as she tightly clenches her fists and pushes down hard into the seat.

"An overdose. She was way too good to survive this place."

She bows her head and her long dark hair veils her face. "Has your mother ever touched your face in such a soft, comforting way that it felt like it had the healing power of God and for the moment all worries were magically removed?"

"Sure, many times," Nick replies.

"Well, that's how Miss Lynch's hand felt. The very next day, I found myself in a dentist chair for the first time. At least half my teeth had cavities but I was lucky. I didn't need braces. All the other girls in our hall did." She smiles and reveals her beautiful teeth as she tries to defuse some of the tension.

The next day, it was a doctor appointment. They told me I was going to have a few minor surgeries, nothing to worry about. I remember them putting a mask over my face and telling me to count backwards from a hundred. When I woke up, Miss Lynch was there. She touched my face and told me that everything went great. I was still so drugged I couldn't talk.

When I finally came to, Miss Lynch told me that I had a few cysts removed from my vaginal area … that it was normal for girls my age to have them and best to get rid of them as soon as possible. And they removed a mole from the back of my neck."

Nicole turns her head and lifts her hair, revealing a surgical bandage on the back of her neck. "I guess this can come off now," she says. "It's been over a week."

She pulls off the gauze and Nick sees a freshly forming scar.

"They put a monitoring chip back there … like the type you might put in your dog. I finally found a doctor I could trust to take it out."

"All the girls had that?"

"Yes. But when you come from nothing and are suddenly fed three delicious meals a day and given beautiful clothes, pedicures and manicures, you don't rock the boat. They gave us dance classes, ballet, taught by real professionals. We swam every morning in a beautiful Olympic-size pool instead of the dirty creek behind our Kentucky mansion. And I was reading a lot … and to my surprise, enjoying poetry. Byron, Keats and Shelly. You'd be surprised what a hillbilly can learn when given a chance. They taught us to speak properly and walk like a lady. I learned how to play the piano and the violin. It was all Mozart and Beethoven, and jazz and the Beatles. No trite country music."

Nicole looks down at her bandage, which has fallen on the seat between them. "I guess you're not a germophobe?"

"No. I've been around enough disease and germs and nasty bacteria in my life that my immune system might be the healthiest thing about me."

"They taught us proper hygiene too. Being pretty was one thing but it was also really important to smell nice. Yeast infections were not a good thing."

Nicole rolls the bandage into a small ball and throws it out the window into the darkness. "*Domus dei, porta caeli,*" she remarks. "The house of God is the door to Heaven."

"They taught you Latin?"

"No, but there were Latin phrases engraved on many of the old stone buildings. Apparently, Catholic monks originally owned the property. *Ex opere operato*."

"By virtue the work performed," Nick translates.

"Very good, Nicky. A Catholic-school alumni?"

"Yeah. So when did the biology classes begin?"

"The very next year … a core requirement. No shame in allowing your greatest asset to be exploited and trashed. After all, ten percent of ten thousand is one thousand dollars and that's not counting off-the-book tips from especially satisfied customers. Not bad for a hillbilly. The training was intensive but thankfully the school had an ample supply of volunteers willing to help explore every aspect of our bodies. Teenage boys, lesbians, middle-aged men, senior citizens … ugly, pretty, disabled. You name it. Actually, you probably would have been an eager volunteer after suffering through all that nonsense Catholic schools preach."

"No, I would not have been an eager volunteer. Some of that nonsense, as you call it, was teaching us the difference between right and wrong … and instilling in us a moral code that I've tried to live by."

"Bullshit. That little speech might work on your mommy but not on a girl like me. If you had seen me in my skimpy lingerie and someone told you to go play doctor, your little brain between your legs would have led you straight to me."

"Not if you smelled like you do now."

She laughs. "Is that the best you can come up with?"

"Let me rephrase. I hope that if I were in such a situation, I would walk away, but not before I kicked the living shit out of the degenerates in charge."

"You would have set me free?"

"Of course I would have set you free."

"And if I didn't want to be set free?"

"They had you that brainwashed?"

"Like I told you, I came from nothing and was suddenly living in a palace. Having my body violated was a small price to pay for never having to go back to that shithole."

"So when did they ship you off to Vegas?"

"When I was seventeen. Young enough to play a cheerleader one night and a socialite the next. Which one would you prefer?"

"The one sitting next to me."

She laughs. "The smelly Nicole?"

"The Nicole from the bar ... before you opened your mouth."

"That's not very nice, Nicky. I've been told I have a lovely voice."

"Was your friend Elizabeth buried in Vegas?" Nick asks.

"God, no! She was cremated. Her ashes are in an urn in my suitcase. When I come across the right spot, I'll set her free."

Nicole looks out the window as she desperately tries not to cry. "You know if I was driving, we'd be there already."

"Patience! Why don't you try to get some sleep?"

"I'm not tired. Why don't you let me drive and you can sleep?"

Nick laughs. "What a coincidence, I'm not tired either. Did any of you girls ever try going to the police or to one of the local newspapers?"

"You really are naïve. What, did you make your fortune inventing some computer game in your mother's basement?"

"Why don't you just answer the question?"

"Law enforcement got fifty per cent off and the sons of bitches never left a tip. As for going to one of the newspapers ... well, let me just say that there's a big desert out there. Vegas might look like Disneyland these days but believe me, at its center, it's as corrupt as ever. Does that answer your question?"

"Yeah, I guess it does."

"So what type of game did you invent?"

"I didn't invent any game."

"So you inherited your fortune?"

"I like to think I earned it."

"But you're not sure?"

"I paid a steep price and no amount of money in the world will ever make up for it."

"So what is it you do, or did, that could make all the money in the world not worth it?"

"That's a discussion for another day," Nick replies as he reaches across the emptiness between them and almost touches her face before suddenly pulling back. "I'm really sorry for everything that you've been through. Truly sorry."

Nicole simply looks at him as he places his hand back on the steering wheel and drives out of the wasteland and toward the City of Angels.

* *

Nick drives down Sunset Boulevard, the glistening lights of West Hollywood in the background and the reclusive, isolated elegance of Beverly Hills in front of him. He turns into the famous Beverly Hills Hotel just above the boulevard and parks in front of the entrance. He gently nudges a sleeping Nicole.

"Wow … we're finally here in just under ten hours," she grumbles.

"Four and a half to be exact."

"Whatever."

A valet opens her door and she gets out. Nick grabs his luggage and hands the valet a hundred dollars. "Just give us a minute, please. We'll take out our own suitcases." He opens the trunk of the car and takes out two pieces of Nicole's luggage and points to a smaller carry-on. "I didn't think you'd want to leave that behind."

She grabs the smaller piece and hauls it out, and he takes one last look at the arsenal of weapons in the trunk, then slams it shut.

"A girl needs to protect herself," Nicole says as a doorman takes her two large pieces of luggage and walks toward the front desk. "Now, is this where you have the manager call you a cab and we say goodbye forever?"

"I don't think so. By the way, what name did you register under?"

"Catherine Barkley," she replies and Nick laughs.

"Interesting name."

"I wouldn't have taking you for the literary type, but then you do understand Latin."

"Sweetheart, I was reading Hemingway when you were still swimming in that dirty pond in Kentucky."

Nicole sighs as they walk up to the front desk and are greeted by the night manager.

"Mr. Righetti?"

"Hello, Joshua. It's been a long time," Nick replies as Joshua walks out from behind the desk and shakes his hand warmly.

"My God, it's been way, way too long. I saw your mother a couple of nights ago eating in the restaurant. She said you've been overseas."

"Yes. Had some dirty business to take care of. Took me a lot longer than I originally thought but thankfully I'm back." Nick turns to Nicole. "This smelly but beautiful creature over here is my cousin Catherine. Just flew in from New York. Had a terrible flight and the poor thing just couldn't stop vomiting."

"So sorry to hear that. Is there anything I can get you?" Joshua asks.

"Yeah, a sharp knife so I can stab this son of a bitch."

"Now, now, Catherine! You're not in the Bronx anymore. Time to act civilized."

"Can you please just check me in? I need a shower and some rest."

"Of course," Joshua replies, walking back behind his desk. He looks down at the reservation sheet. "We now have you staying in a smaller room at the other end of the hotel." He glances at Nick. "Should I move her to one of our luxury rooms closer to the pool?"

"That would be great and put the reservation in my name," Nick remarks as he hands Joshua an American Express Black Card.

"Finally, a reason to keep you around," Nicole remarks.

"That's no way to show your appreciation, cousin."

"Amazing," she replies with a hopeless sigh.

* *

The bellhop leaves Nicole's room and she turns to Nick. "Did you really have to tell him that I couldn't stop vomiting?"

"I had to come up with some explanation for why you smell so bad. The flowers in the lobby were starting to wilt."

"You're a friggin' asshole."

"Seriously. Shouldn't you be saying ... *What a beautiful room! Thank you, Nick.*"

"I've spent the last seven years in Vegas and at least half that time in rooms just like this getting fucked by rich assholes like you. My God, you are going to have to do a lot better than this if you want to impress me."

Nick opens a closet, grabs a laundry bag and hands it to her. "Why don't you go take a shower?"

"Screw you." She grabs a suitcase, walks into the bathroom and slams the door. Nick heads over to the minibar and takes out a cold beer. He drinks it quickly and opens another one as he walks over to the window and looks out at the majestic palm trees towering over the hotel.

A few minutes later, the door to the bathroom opens halfway. "Hey asshole, make yourself useful and put this bag in the hallway." Nick turns as the laundry bag with her dirty clothes hits him in the face. She laughs before closing the door again.

Nick lies comfortably on the couch across from the bed. A clean and refreshed Nicole walks out a few moments later, wearing a pair of Daffy Duck pajamas.

Nick stares at her and looks like he's going to laugh, but suppresses it.

"What? Don't recognize me all clean and not smelling like regurgitated food?"

"It's not that. Just the idea of you wearing Daffy Duck pajamas is a little more than strange."

"I bought these on a whim a couple of days ago. One of the only good memories from my childhood. What were you expecting, a lace teddy?"

Nick smiles. "You look adorable."

She shakes her head, takes a book from her suitcase, and then pulls back the sheets on the bed and jumps onto it. "You know the best thing of all? Sleeping in a big, comfortable bed, all to myself … with no disgusting pig next to me."

"I can understand that."

"So just in case you were hoping for an invitation, it won't be coming."

"I wasn't. What are you reading?"

"*The Sun Also Rises.* Lady Brett Ashley is the best female character ever written. Forget about Fitzgerald, D.H. Lawrence, the Bronte sisters, and Jane Austen. Their female characters are from a different universe. Lady Ashley is a true and honest representation of a woman."

"I like your analysis," Nick remarks as he leans back and closes his eyes. "Enjoy the book."

"It's never disappointed me."

Three

The early morning sunshine touches Nicole's face and she wakes up. Nick's not on the couch, but there's a note:

> *Went for a run. I have some business to attend to afterwards. Take care of yourself. Nick.*

Nicole crumples the little square of hotel stationary and flings it into the trashcan. "So predictable." She gets off the bed and walks into the bathroom, changes into a one-piece bathing suit and pulls her dark hair into a ponytail.

The large area around the pool is empty except for a cleaning crew. The air is hazy and heavy and smells of chlorine, and the palm trees are unnaturally still. The only sound is that of the cleaning crew.

Nicole puts on a swim cap, steps onto a low diving board and plunges into the water. She swims effortlessly, her body in perfect sync as she cuts across the water with barely a splash. She swims for a long time and finally emerges from the water like a golden deity, dripping wet and seductive. She pulls off her cap and unties the ponytail as a tall and slender man in an expensive suit walks toward her. Nicole grabs a towel off the back of a beach chair and starts to dry herself but her eyes remain on the approaching gentleman.

"Nicole? Is that you?" he asks in a heavy French accent.

"Bernard?"

"Yes, Bernard," he replies confidently. "You are even more beautiful than the last time I saw you … more beautiful than all the sunsets this world has to offer."

"Thank you," Nicole replies and sits down in the chair and hands the towel up to Bernard. "Would you be so kind as to dry off my back?"

"But of course. Are you here for business or pleasure?"

"A little of both, but I can always make some time for you."

Bernard glances past her, and she turns to see Nick approaching.

"I'm sorry, *Bernard*," Nick says, "but at the prices I'm paying for this lovely piece of art I'm in no mood to share. You understand?"

"Of course, monsieur. I compliment you on your wonderful taste. Maybe some other time, mademoiselle?"

"Of course. I'm sure my calendar will be opening up very soon."

Bernard bows and walks away, and Nicole closes her eyes and clenches her fists. "I could kill you right now."

"I thought you were through with the profession," Nick says as he sits down next to her.

"I barely have time to take my clothes off before that *batard* is blowing his load. That's an easy five thousand down the drain."

"So there are exceptions … is that what you're telling me?"

She shakes her head. "What the hell are you even doing here?"

"What are you talking about?"

"That was a goodbye note you left on my bed … or did I read it wrong?"

"I don't remember writing goodbye. Come on, aren't you just a little bit happy to see me?"

"Okay, maybe just a little," she admits, "but only because I felt kind of bad the way I treated you after you paid for my room. I even considered cooking dinner for you."

"*You* cook?"

"Of course I don't cook, but I can learn. It's not like I can live forever on four hundred thousand dollars."

"So I was going to be your test subject?" Nick asks.

"I was going to eat it too."

"Oh, I guess that makes it all right."

"Don't be a jackass."

"So how many laps did you swim?" Nick asks.

"I don't keep count. You start keeping count and it becomes a chore. How many miles did you run?"

"Until my body said no more. Did you eat breakfast?"

"I don't like to eat before I swim."

"Afraid you might sink?"

"Just so you know, my stomach is all black and blue where you hit me last night."

"I'm sorry. The next time you put a gun to my head I'll try to remember not to hit you so hard. Is that why you're wearing a one-piece?"

"I always wear a one-piece when I swim, jackass."

"It's almost noon. How about I order pizza from a place that makes pizza that actually tastes and looks like New York pizza? You do like pizza?"

"Who doesn't like pizza?"

"Good. Maybe once we get some really good pizza in you, that frown might disappear."

"Maybe this frown has to do with the fact that I can't explain why you're still in my life."

"Now, now. That's not very nice."

"I just hope it's not because you can't get up the courage to ask me to have sex."

Nick laughs. "Don't flatter yourself. After all, I did see you naked … granted it was dark … but I didn't see anything special or different about your body that I haven't seen on other women."

"Cute! Sadly, I have about a thousand former clients who would beg to disagree."

"Maybe it's just fate that brought us together. You understand that, don't you? It's the underlying message in your favorite book."

"It's pretty to think so."

"Yes, it is."

Four

Nicole steps into her hotel room and closes the door. She leans against it as though expecting someone to knock. Nick promised that he would stay by the pool while she showered and changed. She can't deny that this stranger intrigues her, with his striking looks, and with the kind of easy confidence that most women find irresistible — but she isn't like most women. Her suitcase lies open and she takes out her laptop, but can't get a signal, so slams it shut.

"Fifteen hundred a night and no internet … must be catering to old, *old* Hollywood."

Back at the pool, Nick is sitting in a chair and watches Nicole walk toward him. Dressed in a white slacks and top, she is simply stunning.

"Did you miss me?" she asks.

"You weren't gone long enough for me to miss you."

"Well, when you're as perfect as me it doesn't take long to get ready. And for the record, I didn't miss you one bit, but I'm starving. So where do we have to go for this New York–style pizza?"

They head out the back entrance of the hotel, walk a couple of streets up and stop before a large wrought iron gate. Nick punches in a security code and the gate slides open.

"So is this where the Beverly Hills elite live … behind closed doors?" Nicole asks.

"We all live behind closed doors."

"Wow! That's really deep, Nicky."

Nick laughs as they walk past water fountains and beautifully manicured gardens, and up to the front door. Once again, Nick punches in a security code and opens the door. They enter and Nicole pauses to take in the breathtaking house with its spiraling staircase and sparkling chandeliers.

"Wow! This is really impressive. And yet, you chose to sleep on my couch last night. You must really have it bad for me. You can admit it. I won't think any less of you." She smiles and her eyes sparkle and for the first time Nick gets a look at the teenager before she was robbed of her innocence.

"You're right, I do have it really bad for you and once you walked out of the bathroom wearing your Daffy Duck pajamas that was it for me. I was simply mesmerized and even if I wanted to get up off the couch I just couldn't move."

"I also have a pair of pajamas with Bugs on them. I'll tell you what, if you behave like a good little boy I'll let you see me in them."

"Promise?"

"Cross my heart and swear to God. Isn't that a phrase that you New York boys like to say?"

"Yes, it is." Nick takes her hand and leads her into the dinning area.

"Whenever you get tired of living here, I'll gladly move in, as long as I am allowed to change the security codes."

"I don't live here. I mean, I own the place but before today I haven't been in this house in over three years."

"So who lives here?"

"Occasionally, some very close friends and I suspect my mom might spend a night or two here when she's too tired to drive to the beach. Personally, I'll take our little two-bedroom house in the Bronx where I grew up any day over this bullshit."

"I feel for you," Nicole remarks as they cross the marble floor. "Now, where's that pizza you promised?"

Nick pulls a chair out at the table and Nicole sits down.

"Thank you, sir," she says.

He walks into the kitchen, takes a pizza pie from a large warmer oven and snags two plates with his free hand. He sets everything on the table. "What would you like to drink? Water, a soda, a nice cold beer?"

"How would you like to split a beer?" she asks and Nick laughs. "What's so funny?"

"That's what my mother would always say when we ordered pizza. She's not much of a drinker."

"Well, it's barely noon."

Nick walks back into the kitchen and takes out two icy mugs and a Budweiser from the refrigerator. He pours half into each mug and hands one to Nicole.

"Thank you, sir," she says once again as she picks up a slice of pizza and folds it in half like a real New Yorker.

Nick watches her finish it and guzzle her glass of beer.

"Where did you learn to eat pizza like that?" he asks.

"A New York banker taught me. Why, did you expect me to ask for a knife and fork?"

"Did you even taste it?"

She's already picking up a second slice. "How about we split another beer?"

"Sounds good," Nick replies. He pushes out his chair and heads back into the kitchen. Nicole takes a moment to look around and steadies her eyes on a framed picture resting on a nearby banquet table. She stares at the two ladies in the image, one of them a stunning brunette and the other a pretty, petite blond. When Nick returns, he refills both glasses.

"What, you date Miss Universe for a month or two?" Nicole asks as she points to the picture.

"That's my mom."

"And how many moms removed from your biological mother is she?"

"She *is* my biological mother and the little one is my sister Natalie."

"Wow! It's amazing what they can do with Photoshop these days," Nicole remarks.

"That hasn't been touched up, and it was just taken. In England … see the channel behind them? On their way back from Germany, a couple months ago."

Nicole stands up, still holding the folded pizza in her hand, and walks over to the picture. "Your mother must have the greatest plastic surgeon in the world."

"My mother would never have any work done. That's the way she's always looked.

"I swear I've seen her before," Nicole remarks.

"If you read fashion magazines you've probably seen her a lot. She's been on the cover of every major publication in the world."

Nick walks out of the room and returns with a handful of magazines with his mother on the cover of each one. He shows them to Nicole who looks through the magazines with intense interest.

"How old is she?"

"Forty-seven."

"Amazing! You would think with a mommy this beautiful that you would have inherited some of her looks."

"I got lucky in other ways."

"So your fortune comes by way of mommy. Real sweet … wish I had a mom like that."

"My wealth has nothing to do with my mother."

"So what's your secret?"

"It's not important. Why don't you have another slice?"

"I'm lucky I was able to finish two."

"Too bad! I was hoping to split another beer with you."

Nicole sits back down at the table and looks across at Nick. "Why so secretive?" she asks.

"My life is pretty much an open book," he counters. "I would think that an enterprising young lady like yourself would have had the total lowdown on my life and career by now."

"The internet was down at the hotel."

"Well that could certainly impede any type of investigation."

"By the way, do you have a computer I could use somewhere in this palace? I need to investigate a rich stalker hot on my trail."

"As long as you promise not to investigate your next target."

"I promise."

Nick leads her into a large, wood-paneled study that looks more like a library. Each wall is lined with floor-to-ceiling bookshelves holding thousands of books ... some hardcover but mostly paperbacks.

"Okay, please don't lie to me and tell me that you've read every one of these books," Nicole says.

"Every one. My mom, Natalie and I promised each other that no book would go on any of our bookshelves unless they were read by all three of us."

"Impressive! So Miss Universe and little Bobbie are a lot more than just pretty faces."

"Don't call them that," Nick says angrily.

"I'm sorry. I thought I was complimenting them."

"You were insulting them." He walks across the polished hardwood floor to a large, beautifully designed desk in the middle of the room, turns on the computer, pulls out the chair for her and then heads to the door. "Have fun doing your research."

"Hey, I need the password," Nicole calls out to him.

"Why don't you try your favorite Renaissance artist?"

Nicole types in *Raphael* and looks up at Nick in wonder. "Thanks," she says. "And where are you off to?"

"I'm going to look at a movie. When you're finished, take a left and walk straight down the hallway to the last door."

Nicole quickly types *Nicholas Righetti* into the computer's search engine and a mountain of material appears:

Nicholas Righetti, famed Hollywood director, producer and screenwriter, discharged from the Landstuhl Regional Medical Center in Germany...

Hollywood director and producer Nicholas Righetti said to be in critical condition after shielding fellow soldiers and civilians from a roadside bomb...

The reported death of beloved Hollywood director and producer Nicholas Righetti sends shock waves throughout the film industry...

Nicole strolls down to earlier articles as she shakes her head in disbelief. She sighs as she says out loud, "My God! So this is the famous Nicholas Righetti. I knew I recognized the name last night at the hotel desk." She continues reading...

Nicholas Righetti joins the military and is said to be deployed overseas...

Where has Nicholas Righetti disappeared to? Hollywood executives and family members remain silent...

Nicole finally stands up and stretches as her eyes take in the beauty and the wealth of knowledge that surrounds her. She heads down the hallway, glancing at rows of family pictures hanging on the walls, and opens the last door on the left, a screening room that sits about fifty people. Nick is sitting in the middle watching *A Charlie Brown Christmas.* Nicole sits beside him.

"How are you still alive?" she asks.

"I got lucky. The bomb maker was a real amateur and my doctors were professionals. They did a great job putting me back together."

"Let me get this straight ... I've never been to the Bronx, but isn't it like a half a step up from the shithole I come from?"

"I come from a nice neighborhood."

"So you had running water and air conditioning?"

"Yes."

"Wow! You really are a jackass. You make it all the way up from the gutter, without a helping hand from relatives in the business, and you still enlist and go fight for a country that doesn't give a shit about you and a government that only cares about itself."

"I guess I was searching for a higher purpose."

Nicole smirks. "And did you find it?"

"I did save two fellow soldiers who are both married with kids … and a boy who might one day grow up to be a doctor or a teacher and do wonderful things for his country."

"Yeah, and one day I might find my virginity again."

"Your patriotism is quite refreshing."

Nicole glances at the screen. "Do you always look at *A Charlie Brown Christmas* at the beginning of summer?"

"There's no time frame on genius. You know that. Chuck is the most well defined character in all of fiction … in my humble opinion."

"Well, I'm more a Snoopy-type girl."

"Nothing wrong with Snoopy. It might do you well to emulate him."

Nicole shakes her head as Nick reaches over and hands her a package.

"What's this?"

"Ten thousand dollars. The easy five thousand I cost you with your former client Bernard … the two thousand I cost you by forcing you to leave that beautiful outfit you were wearing on the desert floor to have the vultures feed on it. And for the record, you looked absolutely stunning in that outfit. And three thousand for the miscellaneous expenses I promised to pay you for driving me back here."

Nicole looks down at the money, tapping her fingers against the arm of her chair. "You are simply amazing," she remarks as she shoves the package into Nick's stomach. "And I really hope that hurt, a lot."

"Drop the histrionics. Unlike Bernard, I'm not asking for anything in return." He holds the money out to her again.

"I'm not a charity case, but I will be kidnapping my baby sister, Caroline, before my loving parents have a chance to sell her off. Raising her will not be cheap." She takes the money. "That's a promise I have every intention of keeping."

"I know you have a lot to offer. Maybe, if you give me a chance, I can help."

"I'm not going to get you involved in my life. That would be cruel…"

Nicole leans her head back and sighs heavily. "How much pain are you in?"

"If I don't think about it, not much. And if I took my medicine, probably none at all, but the side effects are awful."

Nicole leans forward and rests her arms and her chin on the seat in front of her. The closing credits for *A Charlie Brown Christmas* roll off the screen as Nick pushes aside Nicole's hair and looks at the incision on her neck.

"How does it look?" she asks.

"Like it's healing nicely. Does it hurt?"

"No," she replies with a small laugh.

"I do have one small favor to ask of you if you have the time. I have a doctor's appointment in two hours. He'll be shooting me up with a bunch of cortisone and probably won't want me driving. It won't take long."

"No problem," Nicole replies as she sits back, folds her legs and looks into Nick's eyes. "Not a problem."

Five

Nicole turns onto Coldwater Canyon as Nick reminisces about the many times he drove over the canyon on his way to work at the studio after he purchased the house in Beverly Hills. He always left extremely early and for the longest time was accompanied by his sister Natalie. Nick and Natalie always worked as a team, whether they were producing, writing or directing a film. It always bothered Nick that she got so little credit when she was such a major part of their success. She eventually made her contributions known when Nick left the business and Natalie produced and directed two blockbuster films on her own in less than two years … a string he had no doubt would have continued if he hadn't sidetracked her with his ill-fated injuries.

Nicole follows Nick's instructions and turns right onto Ventura Boulevard and enters the lovely and quaint Studio City, one of the few areas of Los Angeles that Nick truly loves. It's like a different world from Beverly Hills, Brentwood, Bel Air and Malibu. It doesn't reek of Privilege and Wealth. The houses are one and two stories, mostly colonial, with small yards, nicely manicured … and with actual children playing throughout the neighborhood. Nick and Natalie often talked about buying a house in Studio City or the adjacent Toluca Lake, but that's off the table at the moment … if not forever.

Nick did a fairly thorough search on Nicole, back at the house after leaving her room, and virtually nothing came up. No bank records, no social security number, not even a driver's license. The only thing that made him believe that she wasn't using an alias was that a Nicole Tyler and an Elizabeth Porter rented the same apartment in Vegas for nearly seven years. The owner of the complex described Nicole perfectly and was grief stricken over the death of Elizabeth. The company that Nicole worked for did an amazing job of keeping their talent off the radar.

Nicole is quiet throughout the ride and Nick knows that this does not bode well. She, undeniably, has other targets on her hit list and it doesn't take a genius to figure out that at least one of them is right here in Hollywood. Nick knows that any one of his former associates could be on that list, and he also knows that she is the most dangerous type of assassin. Her outrage is totally justified and her thirst for revenge is not going to dissipate with time or be bought off with money.

They drive past the major studios in Burbank. "Feeling a little nostalgic?" she asks.

"I have a lot of good friends here. Wonderful, creative people…"

"Yeah, and how many of these wonderful people came to visit you when you were on your deathbed, or were they too busy cozying up to your beautiful sister?"

"It's a lot more complicated than you think."

"Is that so," Nicole remarks as her eyes dance across the movie billboards advertising upcoming releases. "So, when did the creative spark that made you so rich burn out … before or after the blast?"

"It's still there. Actually, the whole ride over here I've been thinking about writing a script … a psychological thriller … about a psychotic paranoid assassin."

They glance at each other.

"Doesn't sound like much of a blockbuster," Nicole says.

"I could always use a write-off."

"So is that what I am to you ... a write-off? A pathetic charity case?"

Nick shrugs his shoulder and remarks, "It must be really difficult to live a life where you see everything as a threat. Doesn't give you much time to enjoy the simple pleasures."

"You have it all figured out, don't you?" She parks in front of the doctor's building. "Pick you up in like an hour?"

"Why don't you park in the garage?"

"I'd rather drive around and look at all these glorious studios and their decorative water towers."

"If you're that interested in the history of Hollywood I could give you a personal tour."

"You'd do that?"

"Yeah, and if you behave, I might even buy you a souvenir."

Nicole drives into the garage and parks. They get into the elevator and Nicole snuggles up to Nick. "Tell me, my little baby boy, the real reason you want me to go with you is so I can hold your hand while the nasty doctor sticks you with those big needles."

"I'd be a real fool if I said otherwise."

She runs her fingers across the top of his chest. Nick stands his ground, looks down at her and smirks. "Not quite there yet, are we?" he says, gesturing to a pizza stain on her blouse.

"Well, we still have time to practice ... unless of course you want to take me out on a real date to a fancy restaurant and serenade me over oysters, steaks and champagne."

"We can definitely do that."

"Not afraid being seen with me might tarnish your Boy Scout reputation? After all, I might run into a former client or two."

"Surely, you don't think they'll remember you?"

She laughs as the elevator door opens and they walk down the hall to Dr. Ronald Cotlair's office.

* *

Dr. Ronald Cotlair, a middle-age specialist with a gray, receding hairline and a neatly trimmed beard, looks up at Nicole as she hovers over his shoulder. With Nick waiting in a separate room, Nicole takes this opportunity to look at an image of his injuries on Dr. Cotlair's computer. As she leans in, the doctor cringes and taps his fingers repeatedly against his desk.

"Remind me again, why you're here?" Doctor Cotlair asks Nicole, his strong Brooklyn accent matching his directness.

"I told you, I'm Nick's ride."

"I get that, but usually someone's ride remains in the waiting room ... especially when that person is not a close relative."

"I'm here to provide support and comfort ... to hold the poor child's hand."

"The poor child jumped on a bomb. For some reason, I don't see him needing someone to hold his hand while I give him three shots."

"Apparently, you don't know your patient as well as you think. Anyone stupid enough to jump on a bomb is psychologically unstable and needs all the support he can get." Nicole points to three red dots on the computer screen. "Is that the damage? Is that where you're going to inject him?"

The doctor taps more rapidly as the cringe hardens.

"Fine, don't answer. Be rude. See if I care. I just don't understand why you wouldn't go ahead and zap all the nerves in that area and block their connection to the brain?"

Dr. Cotlair looks up at her. "Because I prefer not to paralyze my patients. Are you a WebMD enthusiast by any chance?"

Nicole waves him off. "I read it in the New York Times. Kill the nerve that's causing the pain. Simple enough."

"No, not simple." Dr. Cotlair remarks, nods his head, and laughs. "Apparently, you're a very smart young lady. Why don't you apply to medical school if you're that interested in medicine?"

"Because that would require that I finish high school and I simply don't have the time. Sadly, I wasn't fortunate enough to be raised in a loving household like you and Nicky."

Dr. Cotlair rolls his chair back from the desk and stands up. He takes his thick-framed eyeglasses off and cleans them with a Kleenex.

"You have a real problem with women, don't you?" Nicole asks him.

"I have two daughters and a lovely wife. Why would you even suggest such a thing?"

"Because you've been nothing but rude to me since the moment we were introduced."

"Maybe it's you … or to be more specific, your motives."

"My motives? For your information, the boy wonder latched himself onto me."

"That's what every successful con artist wants you to believe," Dr. Cotlair remarks as he reaches into a sterilized compartment and takes out three large needles. He fills the needles with cortisone and turns toward Nicole with one in his hand. She looks at the needle as her eyes glaze over. "Maybe you would like to give the first injection?" She wobbles as she reaches out and tries to grasp onto something. She faints as the doctor grabs her before her head slams against the floor.

He places a pillow beneath her head, checks her pulse and breathing, and then picks up the three needles and walks into the adjacent room where Nick lies on his stomach covered by a blanket.

"Your girlfriend just fainted."

"At the sight of the needles?"

"Yes. She's okay. Would you like me to wake her up?"

"No, no. She's a lot less dangerous when she's asleep."

Dr. Cotlair pokes around Nick's back with his hands. "Feels totally numb?"

"It feels wonderful," Nick remarks as Dr. Cotlair picks up a needle.

* *

When Nicole wakes, Dr. Cotlair is there to help her to her feet.

"Wow! Did I faint?"

"Yes, you were quite gone. How do you feel?"

"Okay. I guess this rules out a profession in medicine. Where's Nick? Is he okay?"

Dr. Cotlair looks at her thoughtfully and his tone is softer when he answers. "He's fine. He's getting dressed." He hands her a cup filled with orange juice.

"And did it work?"

"Hopefully, but we really won't know for at least a few days ... and maybe not even then. Nick is not the type to complain."

Nicole shakes her head and smiles faintly. "Definitely not the type."

"But, at least for a few more hours, I can guarantee you that he won't be in much pain. He's still numb from the anesthesia."

Nicole begins to walk toward the adjacent room, but Dr. Cotlair's words stop her. "Tread softly. There will always be someone watching and the consequences may be painful."

Nicole turns back to him. "I've been hearing that warning my entire life," she says.

Six

Nicole stops at the red light at Hollywood Way and Riverside Drive where delightful characters depicted across the Warner Bros. Water Tower look down at the passing traffic.

"So did you and the Doc get along wonderfully?" Nick asks.

"Yeah, if you discount his rudeness and not-to-subtle threats on my life."

"He's doesn't like anyone intruding on his personal space."

"Oh, was that it?"

Nick looks up at the water tower. "Do you still want that tour?"

"Not today. How do you feel?"

"Pain free."

"That's great," Nicole says with a smile.

Nick looks out the window at Bob's Big Boy and the Garry Marshall Theatre at Toluca Lake. "We're passing some very famous landmarks," he remarks.

"Is that so? And all this time, I thought I was sitting beside the only true landmark this town had to offer."

"That's sweet, Nicole, but you know better."

"Do I?" she asks with a touch of contempt.

Nick reaches over and caresses her face.

"Do that a few more times, Nicky, and I'll have to charge you five thousand, and that doesn't include any fireworks."

Nick leans back in his seat and asks, "No discounts for friends?"

Nicole laughs as she stops at another red light. She looks at Nick and softly caresses his handsome face. "I could so easily see you as a heartthrob. Ever think of moving in front of the camera, instead of remaining behind?"

"No!"

"It's not your style, is it?"

"No, it's not. And besides, I can't act." He looks out the window and continues giving directions.

"Make a left here and a right two blocks down. I like going through the residential areas of Studio City and it's just as quick to Coldwater Canyon."

A few moments later, they're driving down the enchanted tree-lined streets that make up most of Studio City.

"It's different around here," Nicole says. "So different from the pompous bullshit you find in Beverly Hills and Vegas. Is this where the not so rich live?"

"There are plenty of very rich people that live around here. They simply don't choose to live behind fences and tall walls; they appreciate the simple, less flamboyant architecture that you find in places like New England. Can you pull over?"

Nicole parks alongside a beautiful two-story colonial-style home, painted white and blue, and with young children playing on the front lawn.

"And now what?"

"I have a proposal for you."

"I'm listening."

"You give up this payback tour that you're on and I—"

"I'm not on any—"

"Don't insult my intelligence. I know exactly what you're up to."

"Well then … since you know it all, you should know that nothing is going to deter me. Nothing!"

"I will have your baby sister in your arms in less than a week. I'll buy you a home anywhere you like … California, New York, Vermont, Paris … anywhere. And I'll round off the four hundred thousand you supposedly have to a million."

"Are you this generous with all the hard luck cases you run into, or is my case so unusual that you can't resist trying to save me?"

She looks away from Nick and stares at the children playing in front of the house. Nick reaches over and turns her face back toward him and looks into her misty eyes. "It's not that your case is so unusual, but you, you Nicole are special."

"My God, you really have fallen hard for me. I never should have let you see me in those Daffy Duck pajamas."

"Don't forget, you promised to let me see you in your Bugs Bunny pajamas."

"I might have to reconsider that promise. If you see me in my Bugs pajamas you might completely go to pieces."

"I went to pieces the first time I saw you walking across the floor at the Venetian."

"So have a thousand other men. The only difference is that you won't let go and you want something from me that I am unwilling to give, at any price. I would think that of all the people I have ever known, you would understand. Elizabeth was my only family. She was without malice. We had our whole life planned out once we left Vegas, and it was going to be beautiful."

"I have no doubt about that, but do you really think she would approve of your current plans?"

"I was her protector, her guardian angel." She puts two fingers close together and remarks, "We were this close, this close."

"I understand, I truly do. But there are other factors, such as your sister. If something goes wrong with your plan, what becomes of her?"

"Please, don't do this. Please," Nicole begs. She shakes her head and tears start to flow down her face. "Now I'm the one going to pieces." She pulls out tissues from her purse and cleans her face. "I am sure of one thing and that is that she would approve of you. I can almost feel her tapping my shoulder and saying, *Look, Nicole, you've found your prince charming.*"

Nick reaches over and kisses her softly on her lips. She kisses him back and they kiss passionately for a long moment as the children playing outside stop and look at them. "We're being watched." Nick looks over his shoulder at the children and remarks, "Sometimes walls aren't such a bad thing."

She laughs as she runs her hands through his dark, wavy hair.

"It really is a pretty little neighborhood, but I need to get back to the hotel."

"I guess that means no to my proposal," Nick remarks.

"Please, don't be mad. We'll always have this moment. It's the first time I've kissed a man and felt real love on the other end."

Nicole shifts into drive and pulls away. The sun is shining brightly and its glow touches Nick's face, yet his body, still numb from the anesthesia, shudders as though an unexpected chill has breached his psyche. Except for an occasional direction, they remain silent.

Nicole parks the car in front of Nick's front door. He insists that she comes in, and after a few impatient remarks and frustrated sighs, she walks into the house with him. She sits and flings her small handbag onto the dining room table and looks closely at him. "You look awfully pale. Are you not feeling well? Want me to call the quack and tell him he screwed up?"

"I feel wonderful. Why so irritated?"

"Because I have things to do, Nick. I didn't break free from my bondage in Vegas to become your personal slave."

Nick picks up Nicole's handbag and takes out her magnetized hotel key. He bends the plastic card multiple times and throws it down beside her. "You won't be needing that anymore. Your room at the hotel has been vacated and I had all your possessions moved to the second-floor bedroom upstairs, overlooking the pool."

"What the hell?" Nicole picks up the mangled hotel key and throws it at him. "Who do you think you are?"

Nick reaches into his pocket and takes out a piece of paper with a Las Vegas phone number scribbled on it. He hands it to her. "Look familiar? Your ex-client Bernard made the call shortly after he left the pool area. Or was that part of your plan? Get a few members of the organization down here and have a shoot-out at the hotel?"

"Don't be ridiculous" She crumples the piece of paper into a ball and rolls it down the table. "And you think I'm safer here, just a few blocks from the hotel?"

"A lot safer here than if you were in your hotel room."

She taps her fingers against the table and remarks, "So you feel wonderful ... that's great. Why don't we split a beer to celebrate?"

"Are you okay?" Nick asks.

"I will be. But for the moment, why don't we concentrate on you?"

Nick looks suspiciously at her, but her eyes remain on the piece of paper.

"I'm thirsty, Nicky. Please go get the beer."

Nick stands up and walks toward the kitchen, glancing back at Nicole who continues to tap her fingers against the table as she looks down at the rolled-up piece of paper. He opens the refrigerator, grabs a beer, and pours it into two chilled glasses. Glancing around the kitchen at the large, cherry cabinets and polished marbled sink, his eyes momentarily come to rest on a bunch of little notes stuck on the refrigerator door — reminders from years ago about doctor appointments, movie premieres, travel dates, and restaurant reservations. He smiles as he walks out of the kitchen and hands Nicole a glass.

"Thank you, kind sir." She taps her glass against Nick's glass. "To feeling wonderful."

She drinks a good amount. "Now, that tastes good and I'm not much of a beer drinker." Nick takes a small sip from his glass and places it on the table.

"How about a slice of cold pizza?"

"Yeah. I'm not the type who counts calories."

Nicole looks over her shoulder at Nick as he walks into the kitchen. She glances at the picture of Nick's mother and sister on the banquet table, and then slips her hand into her handbag and takes out a pill bottle. She opens it and drops a pill into Nick's beer and softly says to herself, "There's no other way."

Nick returns with the pizza and hands her a slice and asks, "Did you just say something?"

"No! Just talking to myself. I admit it, occasionally I do carry on conversations with myself."

"A telltale sign that you should be working in the movie business."

"Are you offering me a job?"

"Yes, an added bonus if you accept my proposal."

"Behind the camera, of course?"

"That's up to you."

"I could easily ruin your stellar reputation."

"Why don't you let me worry about that."

She takes a bite of her pizza, "You know, New York style pizza is one of the few foods I like cold almost as much as hot."

"You sure you don't have some Italian blood in you?"

"I'm pretty sure. I doubt my parents even know what an Italian is. Probably think they're some type of an Iranian."

Nick laughs as Nicole eats her pizza. "Is New York City really as exciting as everyone says?"

"You've never been?"

"No!" She points to the scar on the back of her neck. "Before yesterday, I've never been anywhere but Kentucky, the monastery, and Vegas."

"I imagine you would love it."

"Easy place to remain invisible?"

"Yes, if you choose to be."

She laughs, "Like I have a choice."

Nick softly taps the table as he keeps his eyes glued on Nicole while she finishes her pizza. "Another slice?"

"No, thank you." She picks up her glass, smiles, and says, "Cheers!" They finish off the beer in their glasses.

"I think I'm going to go take a nap ... unless you don't feel good and I can stay down here..."

"I've told you, I feel wonderful."

Nicole stands up and walks toward the winding staircase that leads to the second floor. Nick watches her for a long, chilling moment before getting up and following her. "Nicole!"

She turns, holding onto the banister, and looks down at him. "Yes."

"What's going on?"

"I'm just tired. And besides, I have a lot to think over. That offer is starting to look better all the time. My baby sister in my arms within a week ... a house anywhere I choose ... and a cool million dollars?"

"More like a cool six hundred thousand to go along with the four hundred you already have. It's still on the table ... as long as you don't do anything violent."

"And the house will be in my name?"

"And big enough ... in case you want to throw a little dinner party for the neighbors."

"And you can get me a job in New York at one of the movie studios?"

"Yes."

She turns back around and continues to walk up the staircase. "Like I said, a lot to think about."

Nick watches her disappear up the stairs. He suddenly runs up a few steps and stops. He sighs as he leans against the banister. "She would make a wonderful actress but she has a lot to learn." He covers his mouth as he yawns. He shakes his head and walks back down the stairs.

Nicole walks into her room and takes in the luxurious surroundings — a Victorian king-size canopy bed overlooking the large pool below, and a mahogany executive desk scattered with books and writing tools sitting under another window. Framed pictures of family and friends decorate the walls, and a leather couch and chairs flank the room's grand fireplace. On the far wall, double doors lead into a separate bathroom that's the size of many one-bedroom apartments. Nicole shakes her head and sighs. "And he left all this to go fight a war half way around the world, in Iraq, for a country that doesn't give a shit. And now he's hooked on a whore with a possible bounty on her head. Surely, Miss Universe and baby sister won't be too thrilled about that."

She looks at a picture of Nick on the set of a movie. "And I'm hooked on him ... but a fat lot of good that'll do either of us."

She looks down at her luggage stacked at the base of the bed; nothing is missing. She picks up her laptop and clears a place for it on the desk, then logs in and waits. When she opens a file named "The Company," a road map of Beverly Hills appears. Highlighted in bold letters is the house of movie mogul Evan Thomas ... just a short distance from the Beverly Hills Hotel and Nick's house. She studies the map as a devious little smile crosses her face.

Nicole opens a piece of luggage, searches under her clothes and grabs a Maxim 9 semi-automatic handgun with a fifteen-round magazine and a built-in silencer — a hi-tech firearm that looks like something from a futuristic movie. She slips the gun into her handbag before she starts to undress.

In only her bra and panties, she sits on a chair in front of a full-length mirror and laughs at the idea that she might have some Italian blood in her. Her body is so dark that she could easily pass for a girl from southern Italy. It never occurred to her before, but when Nick introduced her as his cousin, it was no great leap. She applies a heavy layer of white makeup and red lipstick to her face and lips, undermining her natural beauty with unnatural products and giving herself a geisha-like appearance. She had played many roles before and this was just another one ... possibly her final one.

From another bag of luggage, she takes out a pair of black leather pants and a matching top, and slides them on, quick and easy, like an Olympic gymnast. She pulls out a blond wig, takes a few moments to comb it, then lays it carefully on the bed next to a pair of black high heels. Finally she scoops her old clothes and shoes off the floor and drops them into an overnight bag, along with makeup remover. She glances at the clock on her phone and sits back down at the desk and has another look at the map to Evan Thomas's house. She shuts the computer and glances at the phone clock again.

She sets the black high heels and wig on top of her clothes in the overnight bag and slips out of the room barefoot. Halfway down the stairs, she stops. Could the sleeping pill mixed with the anesthesia and steroids hurt Nick? Dammit. She never thought of that. She sneaks through the house and into the movie theater — *A Charlie Brown Christmas* again. A shadow is slumped on a seat in the middle of room. In a second, she's behind him and touches his shoulder. "Nick."

He barely opens his eyes.

"It's not very nice to fall asleep while watching Chuck. Actually, I think it might be a crime."

He smiles weakly and closes his eyes again.

"Oh is my little Nicky tired? It's been a long day. Sleep, sweetheart." She kisses him on the forehead and slips out of house and into her car.

Seven

Evan Thomas made his fortune the old-fashioned way. He inherited it from his rich family back east. They were major players in the retail business and were often mentioned in the Fortune 500 as one of the richest families in America. He was an ungainly child and a troubled teenager, and even though he was invited five different times down to the draft board during the Vietnam War, he managed not to serve a single day. His family were major donors to the Democratic Party, so why should their son serve when there were millions of men … who never paid a penny in taxes … whose lives were dispensable … who would never really be missed. In truth, it was probably best that young Evan never served because he was the type who would throw a fellow soldier in harm's way while he hid in the bushes.

Evan, like his father, was a sexual pervert. His mother, a former fashion model, was a closet drunk. In the twenty or so years he lived in the family mansion, he never once remembered daddy and mommy sleeping in the same room. His father often entertained young ladies in his private study and on occasion, he allowed young Evan to watch him seduce and have kinky sex with girls who were barely out of grade school. Occasionally, after daddy was finished with a certain girl … and if she was sufficiently passed out from the drugs and alcohol he fed her … he would allow young Evan to take a shot at the comatose child. Evan could never last very long at his tender age and his father would laugh at him, sipping a 36-year-old scotch, while listening to Sinatra in the background.

Young Evan loved and idolized his father and aspired to be just like him as long as he didn't have to follow him into the family business. After all, Evan was barely able to finish high school and if not for his father's generous gifts to Evan's teachers, he never would have graduated. Daddy knew it was best that Evan's older brother and sister took over the business. Evan loved the movies and once he was safe from ever being drafted again, he moved to Hollywood. After all, where better to learn how to be a leading man and not worry about any repercussions for raping, sodomizing and drugging young ladies. Yes, it was a perfect match except for the fact that Evan had absolutely no acting ability and could never remember his lines and often during an audition, wet himself. It was truly embarrassing and young Evan swore to himself that one day he would get even with the casting agents who laughed and made jokes about him behind his back.

In a stroke of genius, he decided to become a producer. And with thirty million dollars in the bank, people stopped laughing and began listening to everything he had to say. In a famous Hollywood restaurant, he met a young director/writer who was peddling a script about the five mafia families in New York. The script was rejected by all the major studios in town, and in another stroke of genius … or more likely luck … Evan produced the film with his own money. He put up ten million dollars and the film eventually went on to be the biggest box office smash since *Gone with the Wind*. It won seven academy awards, including Best Picture, Best Actor and Best Director, and that ten-million-dollar investment suddenly turned into a fifty-million-dollar payday. Even Daddy was proud of his son who he honestly felt would never amount to anything, least of all a legendary Hollywood producer.

Evan followed his initial success with a series of critically acclaimed and box office successes. He was nicknamed "Stellar" by the Hollywood press, and in a town where prestige and status are so important, he was given the front tables at the best and most famous restaurants in town — the Palm in West Hollywood, the legendary Dan Tana's and of course, the Polo Lounge inside the Beverly Hills Hotel. He was sitting across from movie icons like Richard Zanuck, Tom Mankiewicz, David Brown and Orson Welles but unlike them, he had never finished reading a screenplay. It was all in the pitch when it came to the young Evan Thomas. Five intriguing and provoking lines from a writer, director or an agent and he was sold.

He was named the head of a major studio but after a few years and numerous box office flops, he was forced to step down. Apparently, his gut feelings and luck had run their course ... at least for the moment. At a hastily arranged news conference, in which he was barely coherent, he expressed gratitude to the oil company that owned the studio for the opportunity to run such a Hollywood landmark and later went on to say that his measly salary of half-a-million-dollars a year was nothing compared to what he made as an independent producer, suggesting that he was underpaid for green-lighting so many movie projects that ended up as major flops.

Despite his box office failures and declining reputation, life was still wonderful for Evan. He purchased a mansion in Beverly Hills and named it after a Roman goddess. He developed a healthy fifty-thousand-a-week cocaine habit and had a harem of young girls, barely out of high school, parading around the house. He performed reprehensible sexual acts on the girls but like a real professional, he promised them all parts in his upcoming movies so they never went to the police. After all, you can take a shower and wipe the piss and poop off you but you can never wash away the shine on your star on Hollywood Boulevard. He threw parties almost every night and many of the Hollywood elite ... actors, directors and fellow producers continued to show up. He still had plenty of money and as long as you had money, you were always a player and where else could you get such young pussy and not have to worry about going to jail?

Evan's love of movies never faded and he opened his own production company and named it "Stellar Productions." The first few movies he produced were modest hits and that was great since he was the sole financier and his lifestyle demanded a steady flow of income. Unfortunately, the hits were followed by a new streak of box office flops culminating in a disaster about a Harlem nightclub during the 1920s, starring two miscast actors and directed by a talentless egomaniac without any qualms about going over-budget.

But Evan was still a wealthy man, though no longer a member of the hundred-million-dollar club ... or even the fifty-million-dollar club ... or for that matter, the twenty-million-dollar club. Like a true survivor, he adapted. Instead of investing the lion's share of his own money in a movie, he enticed wealthy, outside investors with his grand visions. After all, who doesn't want to be in the movie business, surrounded by celebrities and going to premieres where your name rolls by on the final credits, if only for a split second? The parties continued and the cocaine flowed, but the girls weren't as plentiful and the Hollywood elite decided he was too dangerous to be around. His speech was slurred and he started wearing a pair of large sunglasses day and night, indoors and out, that were clownish to say the least. He started keeping his hair slicked back like Rudolph Valentino and his hair tonic, or ghetto grease as people would call it behind his back, smelled like cat urine. He hired a well-known publicist to send out invitations to all those non-Hollywood millionaires — businessmen and women, lawyers, gangsters, and upper-class criminals, enticing them to invest in his latest project, a surefire mega-hit based on a classic TV series from the 1960s starring Roger Moore. Remakes and sequels were the new big thing in Hollywood ... less risk, less originality and what better way to show your appreciation for a piece of art than by defaming its creators with cheap and talentless facsimiles.

Evan and his surrogates did most of their fundraising at parties. First, get the guests a little drunk, offer them hits of cocaine passed around by beautiful young men and women dressed in skimpy attire, and then hit them with the pitch: a five-minute clip, narrated by the Stellar Boy himself, offering his guests the opportunity to enter the glorious world of Hollywood on the back of the most famous producer since David O. Selznick. Naturally, the money came pouring in. So much so, that Evan went over his goal after just two parties, but like a true champ, he didn't stop there and continued with the parties and fundraising. It was so much easier than going to one of the studios and begging for money, not that any studio would give him a single cent. It was at one of these parties that a young, well-spoken man, with a noticeable scar running down the right side of his face, and wearing a dark Armani suit, took Evan aside and made a pitch that Evan could not resist: a charter membership in an organization that would guarantee him, at the very least, a hundred thousand dollars a month for life. The business was buying beautiful girls, age fifteen and younger, living in dirt-poor parts of the country. Once they turned eighteen, the girls would be shipped off to different parts of the country, such as Vegas, Los Angeles and New York, where their services would be in great demand and the large price tag not a problem. Evan loved the idea, and after a couple more hits of cocaine, he wrote out a check for two million dollars. After all, nothing sells like sex…

* *

Elizabeth Porter was born in Appalachia, like Nicole. A God-fearing young lady whose favorite book was the Bible, she was the type of girl who blushed when her friends talked dirty. Unfortunately, she was born beautiful and blossomed at an early age. She believed that God never put a challenge in front of her that she couldn't overcome. So when she was purchased by the organization and uncertain of her future, she never doubted that God would protect her. And when she met Nicole on the plane to New York, she knew she'd found her angel. It was Nicole who wrapped her arms around her and made plans for the life they would lead together once they were released from their contracts or once Nicole came up with a way to escape. They were going to move far away and raise Nicole's sister and never talk about the past. They would decorate for Christmas and have wonderful Thanksgiving dinners. They would be a family, and despite the size of their home, they would always share a room.

Nicole would read verses from the Bible to help Elizabeth sleep, even though Nicole had given up on God and religion a long time ago. Once Elizabeth was asleep, Nicole would often watch her — Elizabeth was her reassurance that the entire world wasn't populated with greedy, selfish, pleasure-seeking individuals. She made a point every day to warn Elizabeth that under no circumstances was she to use drugs. Heroin and cocaine were readily available. Clients were constantly pushing the drugs onto the girls, even though the organization prohibited it. Alcohol, on the other hand, was a constant. Dom Perignon and Cristal flowed freely, often leading to the outlawed drugs. Girls were constantly overdosing. A few were forced into early retirement, their names and lives expunged from the chronicle of human evolution like a wet eraser passing over a dirty chalkboard. And even though Elizabeth would never intentionally disobey Nicole, after a few glasses of champagne, she became susceptible to the persuasive arguments of clients.

The pestilence and filth and disgusting behavior associated with Elizabeth's unlisted profession clung to her, but finally the light at the end of the tunnel was visible. The house with the white picket fence and rose gardens ... filled with unconditional love and the laughter of a child and the rich aroma of home-cooked holiday dinners and beautiful decorations would soon be a reality. Nicole promised.

* *

The investors never saw a penny of their money. The movies were made and they got a chance to walk down the red carpet and mingle with a few stars and see their names flash across the screen, but there was no return. The critics panned all the movies and they flopped at the box office. The well had dried up; not even mailroom clerks took Evan's calls, not even his family back east. But like any good con artist, he took his show on the road. First stop, Las Vegas.

Evan's sole income was from the organization that provided the high-class hookers. The two-million-dollar investment was the gift that kept on coming. Like the greaseball in the Armani suit promised, Evan received a check every month and it was now going on nearly five years since he became a partner. He didn't know much about the organization but he did retain a phone number.

* *

The FBI, IRS, Homeland Security and the local police department all had ongoing investigations into the once famous, award-winning producer. Evan, who had to let go of his legal team, had no idea. As his film career and empire collapsed, his imperial palace deteriorated. Rodents and cockroaches moved in while the young, gullible and beautiful girls packed and went running. The smell emitted by the palace was so intense that nearby residents complained to the authorities. Like a true professional, Evan didn't panic; he used the monthly check from the organization to get a steady high. Sure, the cocaine wasn't as pure as in the golden days, but with enough martinis and a few amphetamines added to the mix, it was like nothing had changed.

Unlike Evan, the organization and its supreme members were quite aware of the situation. They wanted nothing to do with the FBI, IRS or Homeland Security, and if ever there was going to be a snitch, a turncoat, a wheezy little rat … it was this disgusting asshole. And unlike the movies, the cannoli was to be left at the scene.

Naked in his hotel room in Vegas, Evan was snorting coke and drinking martinis, and decided it was time he tried the product he'd invested in five years earlier. He forgot the warning that at no time were any of the girls to be used for one's personal pleasures. He called the number and a friendly female voice answered. He insisted that he was a partner in the organization and demanded that a young innocent-looking girl be sent to his room. He was, after all, Evan Thomas, as he repeatedly screamed into the phone — Evan Thomas, Hollywood mogul and legend.

She put him on hold, looked down at his name highlighted in red. The call was made.

* *

The greaseball who initially recruited Evan into the organization just so happened to be on his way from Los Angeles to Vegas when he received a cryptic message … the location of the target and the approximate time he was to be eliminated. The man in the Armani suit was a real professional. The mobsters in charge of the organization raised him. Carmine Costello, one of the heads of the organization, was like a father to him. He was taught to schmooze and kill and bully in a variety of different ways. He never left clues behind him after doing a job, and outside of his bosses back in Chicago, nobody knew much about him. It was only recently that law enforcement learned of him and was able to tie him to a number of murders, and still they did not know his name. When the man in the Armani suit got orders, he did not question them; yet his judgment and aptitude were so well respected that if he decided an order was too risky to carry out in that moment, or that it could expose the organization to problems, he was free to wait for an ideal time, which was usually never far away.

* *

Elizabeth receives the call and instructions shortly after Evan Thomas makes the call, and an hour later, she arrives at his hotel room. He opens the door, dressed in a bathrobe, holding a martini and wearing his clownish eyeglasses. He looks Elizabeth over as cocaine drips from his nose. “You’ll do.” He waves her into the room, which smells like a sewer — whether from the bathroom, the deplorable creature in front of her or most likely both.

Evan lets his robe drop to the floor and lies on the bed naked, wiping his dripping nose with his finger and placing it into his mouth. He looks like a corpse: a charter member of the walking dead, a pompous asshole too stupid to lie down and play dead. Steeling herself, Elizabeth gently passes her hand up along his thigh. The texture of his skin makes her cringe. It is dry and fractured as though he laid out in the desert sun for too long, unprotected and dehydrated — or maybe he was simply the victim of radiation poison or was accidentally placed in a microwave and left to cook on high. She reaches into her purse and takes out a lubricant and rubs it gently around his crinkled genitals but there is no reaction.

Is he dead? She wrinkles her nose at the stench of decay. All that’s left is for maggots to come crawling through his skin, out of his mouth, eating away at his eyes that are covered by those clownish glasses.

He pushes her away as he lowers his glasses and looks at her with eyes so dilated that they look more like tennis balls. “Don’t you know who I am?”

"Mr. Thomas," Elizabeth replies meekly.

"Mr. Evan Thomas. The world's most famous movie producer!" He snorts two large hits of cocaine, wipes the residue from beneath his nose, and licks it off his finger with his lizard-like tongue. "Don't you go to the movies, you stupid little whore?"

"Not much. I don't have the time."

"Of course not. Too busy sucking cocks and taking it in the ass. Isn't that true, bitch? Tell me, how do you like it in the ass? Hard and dry or hard and wet?"

"I don't do that. Nothing anal."

He reaches for his martini on the nightstand and spills half of it. Rivulets of alcohol run down his shriveled and arid body as Elizabeth, a pure and sinless soul caught in the whirlwind of a soulless beast, moves farther away.

He laughs and laughs, "I'm the great Evan Thomas. You don't tell me what I can or can't do."

He starts to mumble incoherently, a decrepit, rabid beast, unhinged and dangerous ... even his fingernails are unnaturally long and dirty like the claws of an animal ready to pounce on some innocent prey. Elizabeth picks up her purse, excuses herself and walks into the bathroom and closes the door. The stench is unbearable as she looks down into the toilet that is filled with a ghastly amount of vomit, blood, mucus and other bodily discharges. She reaches over and flushes the toilet as Evan blasts through the door, takes her by the back of her hair and pushes her face down. He rips at her panties and tries to force himself into her. Elizabeth grasps a metal Kleenex dispenser, rips it off the wall and flings her arm backwards, smashing it against his head. He falls sideways into the bathtub and she grabs the top off the toilet tank and smashes it against his body. Then she pulls her panties up from around her legs. Shaken like a virgin leaf caught in the whirlwind of a dangerous storm, she runs out of the room.

* *

The door to Nicole's apartment rattles for a moment and then is thrown open. Nicole drops her book and stares as Elizabeth runs past her to the bathroom. A moment later, the shower starts. Nicole knocks, but doesn't wait for an answer. Elizabeth is already on the shower floor, knees drawn to her chest, tears mixing with the water pouring down on her. Nicole kneels next to her, picks up a washcloth and soap and gently begins wiping the body of her one true friend ... her only real family.

Between fits of uncontrollable crying, Elizabeth tells Nicole what happened. Nicole offers words of comfort and repeats over and over again that they would very soon be leaving Vegas and starting the life they have dreamed about. She has Elizabeth promise her that she will not leave the apartment, tells her just to stay in the shower and let the water run over her, and concentrate on the beautiful life they are about to embark on. Then she walks into the bedroom, opens the top drawer of her dresser and takes out her Maxim 9. In the business Nicole was forced into, being emotional was suicidal; nothing was more important than having control. But seeing Elizabeth tonight...

She places the gun in her purse and leaves the apartment.

At Evan Thomas's hotel, she enters the elevator alone and watches the flashing buttons on the panel until the door opens. The man in the Armani suit stands there. "Going down?" he asks.

Nicole shakes her head as she walks out of the elevator.

"Hope your luck changes," he says, unexpectedly, as Nicole looks back at him for a long moment. The door closes as Nicole turns down the hallway to Evan's room. She clutches at the concealed gun in her pocket and slows her pace as she hears footsteps and commotion coming her way. Suddenly, a paramedic gently touches her arm and asks her to move to the side. She doesn't hear him with all the commotion. She panics and pulls the gun out of her pocket and then quickly puts it back as a group of paramedics rush toward her, wheeling a semi-conscious Evan Thomas on a stretcher. She glances down at the pig. "What happened?"

"Fell in the bathtub. A guest called and complained about the smell. My God, it stinks in there."

Nicole enters the room and immediately covers her nose. She looks at the soiled bed, the mound of cocaine, then turns and walks back to the elevator.

Nicole parks her black Jaguar and watches the paramedics unload Evan Thomas at Sunrise Hospital and Medical Center. She gets out of the car and walks toward the entrance, then stops. The man in the Armani suit walks out of the ER. Nicole doesn't believe in coincidences, and if she had to kill the pig and his bodyguard, all the better. She waits for him to disappear and then walks into the ER and to the admitting station. The area is empty, except for a few staff members. A nurse greets her, but refuses to tell her anything about Mr. Thomas.

"Take a seat. Or come back later," the nurse remarks without looking up from her paperwork.

Nicole turns towards the seats, then stops. She reaches into her purse for the Maxim 9, spins around and grabs the nurse by her hair. "You don't seem to understand what that son of a bitch did to my best friend." Nicole slams the nurse's face onto the counter and jams the gun against her head. "And unless you give me some information, they'll be picking your brains off this counter for the rest of the night."

With her face distorted against the countertop, the nurse manages to reach over and touch a stack of papers with her hand. "That's his chart. I don't know anything else."

Nicole glances through the chart then presses down harder on the nurse's head. "And the guy in Armani suit who was in here when the patient arrived … what did he want?"

"What guy? I don't know what you're talking about."

Nicole lifts the nurse's head by her hair. "You really need to learn some manners." She pushes her backwards into a row of file cabinets. "And don't bother calling security, unless you want a few more bodies coming through the door."

She walks out of the ER and gets back into her car. It was useless to try anything else tonight, and besides, she needed to get back to Elizabeth.

When she enters the apartment, Elizabeth is still in the shower. Nicole reaches over and shuts the water off.

"Where have you been?" Elizabeth asks.

"Just driving." Nicole grabs a towel and helps Elizabeth to her feet. She gently dries her off.

"Is he dead?"

"No. He's in the ER."

"You went back to kill him, didn't you?"

"And ruin all our plans? I'd never do that." Nicole wraps her arms around her shaking friend. "I love you, Elizabeth."

"I know. I'm such a problem," Elizabeth stammers.

"Don't ever say that. You are the only reason I haven't gone totally crazy." Nicole pushes Elizabeth's blonde hair back from her face and kisses her between the bruises on her forehead. "Come on. You need to get dressed."

Once in her pajamas, Elizabeth sits on the bed and lets Nicole brush her hair.

"You know, if we ever get low on money we can just let your hair grow really long and sell some of it," Nicole says. "There's a huge market out there for natural hair like yours."

"Why would anybody want to buy my hair?" Elizabeth's voice is so quiet that Nicole has to strain to hear her.

"Because it's absolutely beautiful. Most girls would die to have hair like yours."

"I would much rather have your hair." Elizabeth stares blankly across the room, and Nicole's expression tightens suddenly.

"Don't you do this to me," Nicole remarks, leaning her head against Elizabeth's. "We're leaving tomorrow … for good!"

"They'll track us down. They'll kill us. I don't want you to die."

"No one is going to die. We'll have our chips removed and they'll never find us. And our contracts are just about over anyway."

"It won't stop them. They'll make us examples."

"They won't be using anyone as an example. I promise you that."

Nicole gently twists a shiny curl around her fingers.

These locks, which fondly thus entwine,
In firmer chains our hearts confine,
Than all th' unmeaning protestations
Which swell with nonsense, love orations.
Our love is fix'd, I think we've proved it;
Nor time, nor place, nor art have mov'd it;
Then wherefore should we sigh and whine,
With groundless jealousy repine;
With silly whims, and fancies frantic,
Merely to make our love romantic?

"Did you just make that up?"

"That's Lord Byron. Remember we learned about him back in the monastery?"

"No. But that was beautiful."

Elizabeth leans forward. "I don't want to run away. We'll be looking over our shoulders all the time and never be truly happy and free."

"Promise me, you will not do anything stupid."

"I promise … I just want us to be happy and free and away from here forever with your baby sister. I would never do anything to jeopardize that dream of ours."

Nicole hugs Elizabeth and lovingly kisses her.

Eight

Nicole parks a couple of blocks from Evan Thomas's home. She pulls the wig from her bag, sets it on her head and spends a few moments adjusting things until she's ready. One more glance at her computer map. There it is … a large hole in the fence … one she could easily fit through…

It's six o'clock. She puts on a pair of sunglasses, picks up her purse, gets out of her car and starts to walk toward the mansion. Over by the pool, Evan Thomas is mumbling some kind of gibberish. He sits shirtless in a beach chair, a bag of cocaine beside him and a martini in his hand. With his hair greased back and his eyes hidden behind ridiculous glasses, he looks across the murky brown pool that has vegetation sprouting beneath its surface.

Nicole walks right up to Evan who finally notices her as she steps in front of his beach chair.

"Who the fuck are you?"

She smiles. "I'm a gift … from the Joker."

Evan laughs. "I knew Jackson would never forget me. And you must've cost him a pretty penny. Was it his idea that you make up your face like that?"

"Of course, Mr. Thomas." Nicole turns her back to him and runs her hands along her butt, but when Evan reaches over to touch her she turns around and waves a finger in his face. "No touching. Orders from Jackson. Not until you can prove to me that you can still get an erection the old-fashioned way."

Nicole reaches into her purse, takes out a small bottle of lubricant and hands it to him. "Jackson thought this might help."

"Always the prankster, that guy." Evan stands up and pulls down his pants. He rubs the lubricant on his hands, then slumps back into the chair and watches Nicole dance as he starts to play with himself. The setting sun glints off her black outfit as she gyrates in front of him.

"That's a good little boy," Nicole says as she rubs her butt against his decrepit face.

"Come here, bitch."

But Nicole dances behind the chair again. This time, she reaches into her purse and pulls out the gun. Then she slides in front of Evan, the gun hidden from his view. He continues to rub himself with one hand and reaches for her with the other. But again, she waves a finger in front of his face. "No, no, no."

In an instant, she takes aim, pulls the trigger and erases Evan's genitals from the face of the earth. He cowers as blood shoots out like water from a fire hydrant. She grabs him by the hair as his hands and body flail like a fish caught on a hook.

"Remember the girl from Vegas? This is her gift to you, you piece of shit." She shoots him in both his legs. Any sign of superiority or vanity is gone. His face is as white as the cocaine beside him. Nicole grabs one side of the chair and flips it hard. In his unbalanced state, he falls beside the pool. She stands over him, sees the flicker of life still in his eyes and pulls the trigger twice, splatting his brains across the cement. She kicks what is left of him into the muddy pool and unloads the rest of the bullets into his slowly sinking body.

Stumbling away from the scene, Nicole makes her way to the black Jaguar and climbs inside. She's shaking violently and clenching her fists when she looks into the rearview mirror and suddenly starts to vomit all over herself. "Get it together! Get it together, Nicole!" She snaps her head back and drives off without wasting a moment to clean up. She parks in a secluded area off Coldwater Canyon and starts to take off her soiled clothes and the ghastly makeup.

* *

Nick stands pensively before the sliding glass door that opens to the pool area. The room is dark except for the outdoor lights that reflect off the water and into it. He listens to "Nessun Dorma" sung by the young Jackie Evancho. Nicole, dressed in the same clothes she wore earlier in the day, walks into the room and over to the stereo system. She lowers the volume. "What's with the opera music? It's so eerie."

"Sorry if it offends your tastes," Nick replies without turning around.

Nicole shakes her head and lets the remark slip. "How do you feel?"

"I feel fine considering that I've been shot up with enough steroids and anesthesia to knock out a baby elephant. And on top of that, slipped a sleeping pill."

He turns, holding a drink in his hand. "So how did your date go?"

Nicole flops down on the couch, stretches out and rests her head on a pillow. "Turn on the news and see for yourself."

Despite the music, an unnerving stillness descends upon the room. Nick stares down at her. "You're incapable of feeling remorse."

She doesn't blink. "Since you're feeling so much better, why don't you pour me a bourbon, neat. And please, take your time."

Nick sets his drink down. He strides over to the couch, pushes her feet off of it and throws himself down beside her. "You really have no idea who you're dealing with." He grabs her arm and hauls her up. "Now you listen to me, you psychotic bitch ... go to your room and get the laptop you planned this insanity on."

"You're hurting me."

Nick lets go and she gets up, but before she can walk away, he jumps up behind her, hauls her back and pats her down for any weapons.

"Satisfied?" she asks.

"On second thought, I think I'll escort you." He takes her by the elbow and they walk up to her room.

"Why don't you just cut me loose before it's too late?" Nicole asks.

"Why don't you just shut up and accept my help. The way I see it, I'm the only friend you have right now. And if it wasn't for the fact that I personally know what a sick pervert that asshole was I just might cut you loose."

Nicole crosses her room and takes her laptop from the desk.

"You use any other electronic devices?"

"No." She hands him the laptop and they walk out of the room and down the stairs. Nick leads her to an oversized garage that houses a number of high-priced automobiles. He stops before a row of hooks and picks the keys to one of the most expensive sports cars in the world, a 2015 Ferrari F12 Berlinetta. The sleek black exterior with a retractable top looks more like a piece of art than a car. He opens a side cabinet and pulls out a hammer and a blanket. Nick opens the passenger door.

"I'm not getting in there," Nicole says.

Nick places the computer, hammer and blanket behind the driver's seat. "Just get in the car."

"I drive or I'm not going. Having you behind the wheel of a car like this would be like committing a mortal sin."

Nick looks at her in disbelief and then flings her the keys. She gets in, adjusts the driver's seat and steering wheel and turns on the ignition. The engine roars and she smiles as she looks at Nick beside her. "Now, this is what I call a car."

She pulls out of the garage and stops at the electronic front gate.

"Just don't speed," Nick warns.

"Like there's a police car on this planet that could catch up to me in this thing."

Nick touches her on the arm. "Please."

"My God, you're no fun. I can't believe that you, of all people, own a car like this."

"This isn't my car."

"It's in your garage."

"Probably a gift to my mother."

"She likes fast cars?"

"Not that I know of. She's probably never even been in it."

Nicole looks at the car's odometer. "I think you're right. This car hasn't been driven. Well, if no one in your family wants it, I'll be glad to take it off your hands."

"You're such a thoughtful little creature."

"Thank you. I try my best."

The gate opens and Nicole drives down the street and turns right on Sunset Boulevard, heading straight to the beach. Occasionally she hits the gas for a few seconds simply to irritate Nick and feel the power of the beast.

At Sunset and the Pacific Coast Highway, she turns right. The majestic Pacific Ocean, which runs parallel to the highway and straight up the coast for hundreds of miles, is on the left-hand side.

"Just tell me where to stop ... otherwise I'll have no problem driving this baby straight up to Washington State."

About thirty miles up from where they turned onto the highway, Nick has her make a left into a deserted little parking area no more than sixty feet from the water's edge. She shuts the car off as Nick reaches over the seat and grabs the computer, hammer and blanket. The full moon and clear sky provide more than enough light to see as Nick walks down to the edge of the water and places the computer on the blanket and starts to smash it repeatedly with the hammer until he's sure the hard drive is beyond repair and the computer is unrecognizable.

Nicole watches from the car. "My God, you have some serious anger issues." Nick glances at her. "Give me your phone."

"No way. I have all my contacts on this phone."

"Knock it off. You don't need your contacts anymore and you have no friends."

"All my sister's information is on here."

"Okay, you have five minutes to write it down. You tossed the gun, I hope?"

"I'm not stupid. It's in pieces and floating down a number of different sewers in this godforsaken town."

She tosses him the phone. "I have it all memorized, but you owe me a new laptop and phone."

Nick shakes his head as he pulls out the SIM card. He snaps it in half as he walks back down to the blanket. He smashes the phone and card and starts to fling all the pieces into the ocean. Nicole gets out of the car and walks over to him.

"You know, you're polluting, right?"

Nick continues to fling the pieces into the water and Nicole starts to do cartwheels on the sand beside him. Finally she stops, the moon shining down upon them, and turns to him. "Tell me I'm beautiful."

Nick looks at her in disbelief.

"Tell me how beautiful you think I am."

"Haven't you had enough men tell you how beautiful you are?"

"They were all looking at a price tag."

She's staring into the dark waters now, and he stops and looks at her. For a moment, all the broken pieces seem to come together and form a complete picture. She was a child robbed of her innocence, treated like a commodity and stripped of her humanity and identity. "You're beautiful, Nicole. Simply stunning!"

Nicole turns and kisses him on each cheek. "Thank you, Nicky."

Nick shakes the blanket and the few remaining pieces fly into the water, and Nicole, once again, starts doing cartwheels.

Then she lies down on the sand a few feet from him and looks up at the brilliant moon and the stars and starts to recite Edger Allan Poe's beautiful poem, "Annabel Lee." She pauses frequently as her voice breaks with unfiltered emotion:

For the moon never beams, without bringing me dreams
Of the beautiful Annabel Lee;
And the stars never rise, but I feel the bright eyes
Of the beautiful Annabel Lee;
And so, all the night-tide, I lie down by the side
Of my darling — my darling — my life and my bride,
In her sepulchre there by sea—
In her tomb by the sounding sea.

Then she puts her hands out to him. "Help me up?"

Nick reaches down and takes her by the hands and lifts her up and against his body where she rests her head on his chest. They stand there for a long moment … a troubled and unhinged union, a silhouette in the midst of nature's untold beauty.

She finally breaks away. "I'm cold."

They get into the car and Nick looks across at her, but she's staring out the driver's side window at the waves crashing against the beach, illuminated by the full moon and an ever-expanding galaxy of stars. The ocean scent invigorates ancient memories while drowning a cluster of unfulfilled dreams. "She'll always be with me."

* *

Nicole drives through the electronic gate and parks in the garage. When she gets out, she runs her hands along the top of the car. "Think your mother would be interested in a swap? My lovely car for this beautiful machine?"

"That depends, does your car come with the arsenal in the trunk?"

"I'm sure we can work out a reasonable compromise."

"Yeah, I'm sure you can." Nick holds open the door for Nicole and they enter the house.

"Any chance some of that pizza is left? I'm starving."

Nick disappears into the kitchen as she sits down at the dining room table. She sighs as she looks down. Nick places two slices before her as she looks up at him and asks, "What, no beer?"

He smiles and walks back in the kitchen and returns with a beer that he pours into two glasses and hands her one.

"Thank you, sir." He sits down in a chair right beside her. "So I guess that house, the job, my sister and six hundred thousand dollars is no longer on the table?"

"You guessed right."

"Please, don't hate me, Nicky. I couldn't stand it if you did."

"Have I ever insinuated in any way that I hate you?"

She shakes her head like a little girl and remarks, "But at times it's what you don't say that frightens me the most."

He grasps her face in his hands and looks directly into her eyes. "I've seen way too much to waste my energy on such a distasteful emotion. I might not agree with your actions, but I can't argue with the motivation behind them." He runs one finger along her cheek. "You're so beautiful. Who would imagine that such features could actually be a curse?"

"Just think, if it wasn't for my burning desire for a mojito we never would have met, and you wouldn't be burdened with my curse. I would be hundreds of miles away from here by now. Please let me believe it was fate. Don't take that away from me. I know I should have left town after committing that ghastly act tonight, but I had to come back ... back to you. It was selfish and childish, a teenage girl type moment, but I couldn't help myself."

"And I thank God you did come back. It saved me the trouble of tracking you down. Deep down I know that if anyone so much as hurt my mother or sister, I would seek my own revenge, and it wouldn't be much different than your actions."

Nick reaches over and they kiss. “I would have liked to have met Elizabeth. I can only imagine how very special she was.” Nick stands up. “I’ll see you in the morning. If you like, we can go out and get you a new computer and phone.”

He walks off toward the study and Nicole calls after him and he turns back around. “Just so you know, I would never implicate you. I would tell the authorities that you had nothing to do with any of it.”

“I have never doubted that.” He smiles and walks into the study as Nicole taps her fingers on the table.

Nine

Nicole walks into her room, closes the door and lies on the bed, defenseless against the onslaught of thoughts, like the many arms of an octopus attacking her. She looks out the window at the lighted pool as shadows cross the surface of the water. The moon beams brightly and a canopy of stars blankets the nighttime sky. She is tempted to simply jump into the pool and hide deep below the water … forever invisible.

Nick walks by the closed door and hears the unnerving sounds of terror coming from inside the room. He knocks on the door, but by this time Nicole is lost … a prisoner in a nightmarish trance. He enters and immediately walks over to Nicole, who is lying on the bed. As he looks down at her, she stares unseeing with wide eyes, her hands clawing the air as she fights off invisible monsters.

"Nicole." He takes her hands into his warm ones. "Nicole, everything's okay."

Her sweat-drenched blouse and hair stick to her skin. Nick takes a washcloth and wipes the perspiration from her forehead and cheeks. He soothingly reminds her, "Everything's okay. You're safe." She relaxes as Nick runs his hands through her hair.

"You know, I loved the way you recited "Annabel Lee" by the ocean tonight. You just keep on amazing me. Is that your favorite poem?"

"Sometimes ... when I'm by the water. I love Byron."

"Me too. Do you have a favorite?"

"I used to but ... not anymore."

She closes her eyes as Nick gets into the bed and holds her. He whispers, "I will never let anyone harm you again ... never." He rests his head against her sweat-drenched blouse and does not let go. He lovingly recites,

Our love is fix'd, I think we've proved it;
Nor time, nor place, nor art have mov'd it.

* *

The following morning, Nicole wakes up in her outfit from the night before. She puts on her bathing suit and walks down to the pool. As she passes the kitchen, morning noises float through the air. Nick should be up by now, but she doesn't bother to go see what's going on. She needs to get into the pool, to start swimming ... lap after lap like an Olympian, but never with the goal of winning a medal.

Later, she slips a robe over her bathing suit, walks into the screening room and sits down beside Nick, who's watching *A Charlie Brown Christmas* again.

"How was the pool?" Nick asks.

"It was great." Nicole flips off her slippers, turns in her chair, and places her feet on Nick's lap. "Let me guess, you've never been in it?"

"I've been in it."

"A foot massage, please?"

"If you insist." Nick starts to massage Nicole's manicured feet.

"I can teach you how to swim if you like."

"I know how to swim. All part of basic training."

"Oh, I forgot. All in search of a higher purpose."

Nick laughs. Nicole wiggles down into her seat and closes her eyes. "A little more pressure, please. I'm a big girl." Nick pushes harder. "Have you looked at the news this morning?" She asks.

"Yes, it was the lead story and on the front pages of the newspapers. I called the sheriff's office and spoke to the him."

"Why would you do that? Have a change of mind and decide to turn me in?" Nick pinches her butt really hard and she screams. "Hey, that really hurt."

"That's what you get for suggesting such a stupid thing. I asked him if I needed to add protection and security around the house. He laughed and said he was quite sure it was an isolated crime."

"Any suspects?"

"Yeah, he said anyone living in a mile radius of Evan's home. He said over the past six months there have been thousands of complaints about the odor coming from the place. After the story blows over in a few days, it will not be a top priority for his department."

"He told you all this?"

"My family is a big contributor to the police and sheriff departments throughout the city. He also told me that it was the feds's problem. They were the ones really interested in the creep. Apparently, the FBI, Homeland Security, and the IRS were getting ready to arrest him. The FBI was convinced they could easily turn him and have him testify about a mob operation involved with the recruiting of underage girls into prostitution. Know anything about that?"

"No! Someone high up in the organization had to snitch. If I hadn't met you only a few days ago I would swear it was you."

"I'll take that as a compliment. The sheriff reassured me that my family was in no danger. That is the truth, isn't it?" Nicole shoots up and hits Nick really hard in the shoulder.

"I hope that hurt a whole bunch. Insinuating that I could intentionally hurt innocent people." She turns around and lays her head on Nick's lap. "Now, I need a head massage. Gently, please."

"One could never be too sure."

"Keep it up and you are going to find out that I can hit a lot harder."

There was silence until Nicole blurted out the question that had been on her mind since coming downstairs.

"So what went on in my room last night?"

"I don't know. What went on in your room last night?"

"You should know. You were in it … or am I mistaken?"

"No, you're right. I heard you screaming. You were having a nightmare. I woke you up and you went right back to sleep."

"But you didn't leave right after?"

"Nope."

Nicole looks up at him. "And?"

"And nothing. I held you. I rested my head against your body. I stayed until the sun started coming up."

She reaches up and kisses him on the mouth. "I don't remember the nightmare but I did wake up feeling very refreshed … even if my clothes had a terrible stench about them."

"You slept like a kitten."

"Can you still help me get my sister?"

"I thought you had that all planned out."

"I did, then I met you."

"Fate!"

"Yes, exactly."

"Of course, I'll help you. And if you behave, I might put that proposal back on the table … with a few added amendments."

"Such as?"

"We'll discuss that at a later date."

Nicole looks at the screen as Linus gives his famous speech about the meaning of Christmas. "Do you ever get tired of looking at Chuck?"

"Why would you even ask such a question? It's like reading *The Sun Also Rises* over and over again. You can never get tired of such a wonderful piece of art."

Nicole sits up and wiggles herself comfortably onto Nick's lap. "How do you feel? I can't imagine all that hammering last night did you any good."

"You'd be surprised at the medicinal effects of sleeping beside such a beautiful woman."

Nicole places her hand on his face.

"You have a real chance to make a wonderful future for you and your sister."

"Assuming I don't get arrested?"

"I wouldn't worry about that, unless you're planning on some more reckless adventures."

"And what would make you think such a thing?"

"Don't act cute with me. It's insulting. It's time to put your daughter first."

"You mean my sister?"

"The child you're hoping to save from a life that you were forced to live."

Nick gently untangles himself from her and stands up. "Why don't you go get dressed and we can go shopping for a computer and phone?"

"In a minute," Nicole replies.

Nick walks out of the screening room as Nicole watches the credits roll by on *A Charlie Brown Christmas*. Surely she was thinking like a teenager. Of course he would leave her. A girl with her background never got a guy like Nick unless it was in a movie.

Ten

Nicole gets behind the wheel of the Ferrari and starts it up like a kid playing with a new toy. She pulls out of the garage, drives past the electronic gate and turns onto Sunset. "I'll let your mother keep the arsenal in a swap for this car."

"How sweet of you," Nick replies with a smile.

"I think so. So what would your mother think if she knew you were hanging around with a deranged, ex-high-class hooker?"

"And what makes you think she doesn't know?"

"You're joking, right?"

Nick doesn't reply as he looks across at her. She is undeniably stunning.

"I imagine she would go crazy?" Nicole asks.

"No, I don't think so. Some people might argue that she's the last person who should be attacking another person's choices and behavior."

"Why would you say that? Everything I've read about her is simply wonderful."

Nick looks at Nicole's hands gripping the steering wheel like a professional race car driver. Like the car, Nicole is powerful, sleek and stylish, with a commanding presence. But this car has a tendency to break down; it requires continual and expensive maintenance and service. It might be the dream car for many, but it's truly a rich person's car. The car and Nicole might seem like a perfect fit, until one unmasked the very different and irreparable flaws in both of them.

"So, she's not as wonderful as all that?"

"She's more wonderful than anything you've read about her," Nick remarks. "But she has her flaws and when you put her on a pedestal like I have, even the smallest flaws are magnified."

Nick looks out the side window as they drive over Coldwater Canyon. "My mother has never been one to rush to judgment about anyone, and she's perceptive in a way that would have impressed Sherlock Holmes. If you think you can outsmart her, think again. Behind that mask of transcendent beauty is the most intelligent and creative person I've ever met."

"It must have been amazing to be raised by such a person."

"It was. She's infectious and mesmerizing ... a force so powerful that it's nearly impossible to break away from her. Despite my sister's amazing achievements, I seriously doubt she will ever leave my mother's side. Natalie and I used to take her on movie dates with us, which didn't help us much if we were hoping for a long-term relationship with someone. In Natalie's case, a number of her dates fell in love with our mother. I used to feel terrible for my sister."

"I don't understand, why didn't your mother just stay at home?"

"We preferred going to the movies with her than with our dates. My mother's insights and analysis of a movie were fascinating. The discussions we had afterwards were priceless. It was wonderful and yes our dates might not have been too thrilled, but what we learned from our mom are many of the things that made my sister and I so successful.

"*You* broke away from her," Nicole hesitantly remarks.

"Its not like she ever held us prisoners. She's always preached to us the importance of independence, but she is so much more than just a mom. She has always been our best friend. My sister and I are the two luckiest people in the whole world." He looks across at Nicole and the contrast between their families is so overwhelming that Nick lowers his head, embarrassed. "I'm sorry for going on like that, Nicole. I still can't get a handle on the fact that there are parents in the world who could actually sell their children like heads of cattle."

"It's okay. I like hearing you talk about your mom and sister. It makes me happy to know that for all the evil that exists, there is also a lot of good."

"I have no doubt that when you meet them, the three of you will get along wonderfully. They're like you: generous to a fault, loving, caring..."

"Have you already forgotten some of my recent exploits?"

"No, but that behavior is in the past and I don't expect it to be repeated."

"And if your mother and sister don't think I'm so wonderful?"

Nicole parks in the lot behind the electronics store, then freezes at the wheel when she notices a well-dressed, middle-aged man walking toward the entrance.

"We need to go back. I don't need a computer or a phone. You've already spent way too much on me." She starts the car again, but Nick reaches over and turns it off.

"What's is it?" he asks.

"We simply need to go, please."

"No, not without an explanation. You look like you have seen a ghost. Was it the guy who just walked into the store?"

"Yes!" She looks straight ahead, without blinking. "I should have known I couldn't come to a town like this and not be recognized. I should have just done what I had to do and left."

She sighs and shakes her head. "The guy who just walked into the store is a former client ... a repeat client and a real piece of work."

Nick reaches under his seat and pulls out a Maxim 9, similar to the one she used to kill Evan Thomas, and hands it to her. "I think you know how to use this ... If anyone comes toward you and you think they're a threat, you know what to do.

In the meantime, I'm going into the store and buying you a computer and phone."

After he leaves, Nicole puts her head down on the steering wheel and starts to cry. She could not see any way this was going to end happily.

Less than half an hour later, Nick taps on the window and she unlocks the door. He gets in, opens a shopping bag and shows her a new computer, software and a cell phone.

"Can you help me set everything up?"

"It's completely loaded and ready to go. I called them up earlier and had them do everything." Nick replies. He reaches over and places the bag behind his seat. As he turns toward the front, Nicole reaches over and kisses him. They kiss for a long time. "Thank you."

She starts the car up and drives out of the parking lot.

"We're going to have to get you a disguise. A big floppy hat, larger sunglasses, and some baggy clothes, then you might not look so damn stunning all the time."

Eleven

Nicole places the computer and software on the table, then turns toward the front door. Someone is knocking. She calls out to Nick and reaches into her handbag and takes out Nick's Maxim 9. In a moment, he's by her side. He grabs the gun out of her hand and hides it in a drawer inside the banquet table.

"It's family," he says.

He walks to the front door and is greeted by Ava, a precocious nine-year-old who leaps into his arms, and her parents Gina and Frank. Nick takes their suitcases and puts them off to the side, then swings Ava back and forth in his arms. "Oh, I have missed you so much."

Nicole looks at Ava and frowns. Such a beautiful little girl with wavy dark hair, large brown eyes and a perfectly oval face. She looks more like a doll than an actual child; and like a doll, she has probably known nothing but unconditional love and adoration her whole life. The very things Nicole never had.

Nick introduces the family and Nicole greets them with a smile and handshakes. Frank, the family's lawyer, and Nick excuse themselves and walk into the study. Gina takes Ava by the hand and walks into the kitchen. It's apparent that the family has been here many times before and clearly knows the house better than Nick. They come back into the dining room with a glass of orange juice.

"She's been pestering me for orange juice ever since we got off the plane." Gina drops into a chair at the table and Ava snuggles on her lap and hugs her, then sips her juice. Nicole sits across from them with her new computer in front of her.

"How was the flight?" she asks.

"It was great. Flying first class makes such a big difference. I swear, I don't know how people fly coach. So, have you known Nick for long?"

"Not long."

"So, you haven't met Angie and Natalie, yet?"

"No, but I've heard a bit about them."

"Well, you're in for a real treat. As great and wonderful as Nick is, he only makes up one third of this amazing family. Angie and Natalie are heavenly, and we owe them all so much … so very much." Gina holds Ava tightly as tears well in her eyes. "Of course, they don't want to hear about it."

"I have the most beautiful mommy in the whole world," Ava exclaims as she kisses her mother. Then she climbs up onto the table and crawls toward Nicole. Gina grabs her by her little leg. "You know better than to crawl on a table with your shoes on."

"Nick doesn't care," Ava replies, but she sits and unties her shoes, and hands them to her mother.

"And do you think it's any better to be on a table where people eat with your smelly feet all over it?"

"My feet don't smell."

"Everybody's feet smell, especially after they've been on an airplane all day. You should take a bath before we go to the doctor."

"Why? He's not going to check my feet." She pulls her hair away from her ear and shows Nicole a large scar across the lower half of her head. "That's where they cut the stupid cancer out of my head."

Nicole looks at the scar as pangs of remorse and guilt overtake her like a tidal wave. This child has had a hard life too.

"You're so pretty, Nicole. Do you want to marry Nick?"

Nicole blushes and Gina turns red too. "You know better than to ask someone a question like that!"

Ava pretends not to hear her mother. "Because if you want to marry him, it's very important that you love Chuck, Snoopy, Linus, Schroeder, Lucy and the New York Yankees too."

Ava crawls into Nicole's lap and looks intently at the new computer.

"Please forgive my daughter," Gina says. "I think the long plane ride has been a little too much for her. She seems to have left all her manners back in New York."

"It's okay. She's lovely," Nicole says. She touches Ava's hair, twirling it gently around her fingers.

"You see, mommy. It's okay." Ava looks up at Nicole with her big brown eyes. "My beautiful mommy worries about me all the time but I tell her that I would never leave her."

Gina gasps then turns away from them and wipes her eyes on her sleeve. Then she stands up, excuses herself and walks into the kitchen.

"I tell her not to worry," Ava repeats as she starts to press buttons on the computer.

"It's because she loves you so much," Nicole says. She lifts Ava off her lap, stands up and places her in the chair. "Why don't you play with the computer?"

Nicole walks into the kitchen to where Gina is crying in front of the kitchen sink. She puts her hand on Gina's back.

"I'm sorry. My child is a million times more courageous than her stupid mother. I just can't tolerate the thought that…" She stops, pulls her hand away, leans over the sink and vomits.

Nicole grabs the counter next to her. The sudden, unexpected turn of events has left her speechless and images of Elizabeth bombard her.

"I'm going to have to sanitize the sink," Gina remarks, turning on the water. She leans down again, takes a drink and spits it into the sink. Then she splashes some water around the drain until all the vomit goes down. She takes cleaner and paper towels from beneath the sink, but Nicole touches her shoulder and gently moves her away.

"I can do that," she says, and an immediate bond is formed between the grief-stricken women.

Gina watches Nicole clean the sink. "For the last month, I've been praying every day, saying novenas, and all the time trying to put on a happy face…"

"You love her. Every mother should have so much love for their daughter."

"Do you have children?" Gina asks.

Nicole shakes her head. She washes her hands and wipes them dry with a dishtowel. "Do you want some orange juice?"

Gina smiles. "I need something a lot stronger than juice … but that's going to have to wait. Thank you."

Nicole fiddles with the dishtowel in her hands and finally sets it down on the counter. "Could I … would it be okay if I went with you and Ava to the doctor?"

"Yes, of course. It would be so much better than going with my husband, actually. He tries to calm me down and only makes things worse."

They walk back into the dining area where Ava is still playing with the computer. She motions for Nicole to come and look at the screen and Nicole walks over and looks down at Charlie Brown and the gang visiting Snoopy's art museum.

"If you make this your screen saver, Nick will definitely want to marry you," Ava remarks proudly.

"My God, you are not only beautiful but brilliant."

"Yes, a little too brilliant for her own good," Gina remarks as Ava jokingly sticks out her tongue. "If you don't watch out, I'm going to cut that thing off one of these days." She puts her tongue back in and as Gina turns away she puts it back out. "I saw that." Ava laughs.

"How old are you, Ava?" Nicole asks as she gently caresses the child's hair.

"Nine."

"A whole nine. Wow! I'll tell you what; I will definitely make it my screen saver, even if Nick doesn't want to marry me. I can't think of a better picture. Thank you."

"But he will want to marry you," Ava replies with childish certainty.

Twelve

Gina buckles Ava into the backseat of a Chevy Tahoe Truck that's parked beside the Ferrari in the garage. Then she and Nicole sit up front. Gina looks out the driver's side window at the Ferrari. "Wow! That wasn't here the last time we were."

"I would love to drive that, Mommy."

"Maybe in another fifteen years."

Nicole turns to Ava. "I've driven it. It's so much fun."

Ava's big brown eyes grow even bigger. "Can we go for a ride when we get back?"

"You're going to have to ask Nick. He doesn't trust me to go the speed limit when I'm behind the wheel of that car."

"But you're suppose to go really fast. That's why they build them like that."

"Exactly! Don't forget to tell Nick that when we get back."

Gina turns onto Sunset Boulevard and drives west toward UCLA Medical Center. Nicole was taken aback by Nick's less than enthusiastic response when he found out that she would be joining Gina and Ava on their trip to the doctor. He didn't object, but his expression left no doubt that if anything should go wrong, he would hold her personally responsible and the consequences would not be pretty. It was still fresh in Nicole's mind that when she asked Nick, *And if your mother and sister don't think I am so wonderful,* he did not answer. She felt hurt but she understood. It was one thing for Nick to intrude into her life and try to save her, but that didn't mean he trusted her with the people and family he cherished. That trust could only come if she joined a sisterhood of nuns and dressed in an old-fashioned habit like the Ingrid Bergman character in the movie *The Bells of Saint Mary's.*

They enter the radiology department at the Medical Center. Gina signs Ava in and after a few moments they are escorted to a room with a large MRI machine shaped like a tube. Ava remembers the technicians from the last time they were here three months ago and she hugs both of them. They remember her too and have already downloaded the soundtrack to all the Peanuts movies and TV shows. Ava is very excited and can't wait to get rolled into the tube and listen to the music. The technicians fasten the straps around her, remind her to be very still, and in she goes, as her mother and Nicole wave.

Nicole and Gina walk into the waiting room and sit. Tension and anxiety are written all over Gina's face. She drops her head, makes the sign of the cross and softly recites a prayer. She finishes with another sign of the cross and looks back up. Nicole reaches over and caresses Gina's hair like she often did with Elizabeth after a rough night. "Everything is going to turn out great. Snoopy would never let anything happen to her."

Gina laughs.

"Gina, how long have you known Nick and his family?"

"Forever! We all lived on the same block ... just a few houses apart. My husband's family, my family and Nick's. Natalie and I were classmates from kindergarten all the way through high school."

"What was it like? I mean the neighborhood you all grew up in."

"It was really nice. Simple. Working-class. Yet everyone took pride in their homes. Nothing like you see on TV. The part of the Bronx we grew up in was different. There was very little crime ... it was mostly Italian and Irish families. Very Catholic. I wouldn't change it for all the money in the world."

"And where do you live now?"

"You mean when we are not living at Angie's house out here? Westchester, New York ... Angie's family bought us a place. If they weren't so nice and humble I would be suspicious."

"They must really love you."

"Yeah, and my husband is the family lawyer. They're his only clients. It's a dream job. Ava's medical bills have run into the millions and they pay for all of it. Nick and Natalie are Ava's godparents. They could just as well be her parents. There's nothing they won't do for her. Throughout this whole ordeal, it's been Angie and Natalie who have kept me from going insane. While my daughter was having her brain cells destroyed by radiation and chemotherapy, Angie taught her how to read, write and use a computer. And Natalie helped her with her exercises every night. Ava suffered partial paralysis in her left leg because of the treatments, and her speech was very slurred. Occasionally, she still slurs some words. Nick insisted that we relocate out here ... live in the mansion like we owned it ... and made sure she was treated by the best oncologists in the country."

"Does anybody but your family ever live in that palace?"

"Not that I know of, but now that Nick is back he might stay for a while."

"I don't get the feeling that Nick likes that place very much."

Gina smiles. "The house is nothing like the family. It was built for people who don't want to see each other. Their house in Malibu is much cozier, like the houses we grew up in ... except with a wonderful view of the ocean."

"Did much change while Nick was off getting blown up?" Nicole asks.

Gina shakes her head. "It's better not to go there." Then she looks up at a nurse who is walking their way.

"Doctor Grossman is ready to see you," the nurse says.

"Where's Ava?" Gina asks as they follow the nurse down the hall.

"With the doctor. He's a big Snoopy and Charlie Brown fan, remember?"

They enter the doctor's office and take a seat across from a large computer screen. Doctor Grossman enters from an adjacent room and gives Gina a big thumbs up. He turns on the computer and the screen lights up.

"Today, my lovely assistant is going to explain the results. Oh, come on out, lovely assistant." Ava walks into the room dressed in an oversized doctor's coat and picks up a pointer as the doctor clicks the first of three images. She points to three different dark areas around her brain and grins at them. "As you can see, ladies, no cancer."

Gina jumps up and hugs her beautiful daughter as Nicole smiles.

Ava pulls back and looks at her mom seriously. "The doctor recommends two scoops of chocolate chocolate-chip ice-cream for the patient."

"I don't remember recommending that."

"That's because you were too busy talking about Snoopy and Chuck. You wrote it in your notes."

"Okay, as long as you say so. Two very large scoops of chocolate chocolate-chip ice cream for the cancer-free patient."

"Thank you! No more crying, mommy. Promise?"

"I promise."

Thirteen

Gina happily talks on her cell phone as she paces back and forth outside the ice cream parlor. Nicole and Ava, meanwhile, bury their faces in a scoop of vanilla and a double scoop of chocolate chocolate-chip topped with chocolate sprinkles.

"You might want to slow down. It'll last longer," Nicole says.

"I can't help it. I love chocolate so much. Can I have another scoop before mommy comes?"

Nicole can't resist. A few moments later, Gina walks up to them and looks down at Ava's bowl of ice cream.

"Strange, I thought you would be all finished by now. Unless of course, you bribed Nicole into buying you another scoop."

Ava grins up at her with a face smudged with ice cream and sprinkles.

Gina picks up a spare spoon and sits down. "Can I at least have a little bite?"

"Of course," Ava replies as Gina dips her spoon into the ice cream and takes a bite.

When they get back to the house, Nick and Frank are waiting at the front door. Gina wraps her arms around her husband. "Our little girl is doing great." She starts to cry as Frank ushers her into a side room.

Ava looks up at Nicole. "She's never going to stop crying … *because of me.*"

Nicole bends down and gently holds Ava's hands. "You know, people cry for different reasons. Sometimes because they're scared and worried and other times because they're so happy and relieved. Your beautiful mommy is crying now because she is so happy that her precious little girl is okay. I only wish I had a mommy like yours."

Ava hugs her and Nicole holds onto the child as though she's a lifeline until Ava wiggles out of the hug.

"I'll be right back," she says as she runs off. Nicole stands up and sees Nick looking at her.

"What are you looking at? Surely you've seen everything I have to offer."

She walks past him and into the dining area and starts to pack the computer she left on the table. "Is it okay if we use the study?"

Nick follows her to the table. "What's wrong?"

"It's okay if it's just you and me. After all, we know how well you can defend yourself. I still have the bruises to prove that. But when it comes to the people you really love, you have your doubts about me ... not that I blame you. Because when you get right down to it ... all I am is a psychotic little whore who you've taken pity on in order to appease your own sense of guilt."

"And how long have you been rehearsing that little speech?"

She steps back and shakes her head. "It must have been nice to have the world by the balls ... but not even I can imagine how terrible the fall from grace must have felt for someone like you."

"I can assure you, I have no idea what you're talking about."

"And I can assure you, you know exactly what I'm talking about."

"Whatever. And by the way, you should take advantage of the time you spend with Ava. You could learn a thing or two from her."

Nick starts to walk away, then stops and turns back and looks down at her sexy dress. "I thought you were going to dress down when you went out?"

"Is that what you really want, Nicky?" she asks.

"I thought that's what we agreed on."

She reaches down and takes off her high heels and hands them to him. "Is that dressed down enough for you?"

Nick places the shoes on the table and Nicole laughs. "I don't think your mother would approve."

"We don't have to tell her."

"Wow! You just gave me something I can hold over you."

"That would only make my mother suspicious of you and your motives. It's like I told you, she is so much more than a pretty face. She's a girl from the Bronx, and girls from the Bronx are quite adept at reading other people."

"Well then, I have no chance at all with her."

Nick steps toward her again and lifts his hand as though he's going to touch her face, then lets it drop. "Just be yourself, beautiful Nicole, and she'll love you. Be the compassionate girl who reached out to a mother in distress and explained to a child the difference between happy tears and sad tears. Be the girl who gave everything to save her soul mate, the girl who came to check on me after drugging me."

Nicole looks up at Nick with trembling lips and aching eyes. He reaches down and kisses her as the shackles of mistrust are unlocked and the bonds of an uncertain intimacy are formed. Ava walks back into the room and watches as they kiss. She starts to clap as they stop and look at her. "I told you he wants to marry you."

"It's not nice to spy on people," Nicole replies. She untangles herself from Nick and takes Ava's hand. On the way out of the room, she picks up the laptop. "Will you let Gina know we're in the study?"

Nick is standing there, dangling her shoes. She smiles as her face radiates with an unfettered happiness.

Fourteen

Ava's laughter carries across the entire length of the pool and is easily heard by Nick, Frank and Gina who sit under a canopy grilling steaks and burgers and enjoying a few cocktails. A child's laughter can cure many diseases ... mental or physical. Like a wonderful jazz musician, the giggles reawaken a dormant, untarnished heart and soul that once existed in all of us.

Nick occasionally glances across at Nicole teaching Ava the backstroke. She holds onto the child and each time she lets go, Ava sinks and re-emerges, laughing uncontrollably. Nick smiles as he sips his beer. He turns and sees his mother and sister walking out of the house and toward them.

Ava spots them too. She kisses Nicole, swims to the edge and climbs out, then runs dripping wet into the arms of Angie and Natalie. The two women embrace the joyous child. Gina, Frank and Nick stand up and greet them. Gina reprimands Ava for getting the two ladies all wet and Angie laughs as she picks the child up and holds her tightly; Nick's mother is so beautiful and classy that not even a wet outfit can distract from her magnificent aura.

Nicole promises not to hug anyone with her wet bathing suit on and she shakes their hands, then puts on a robe and sits with the rest of the group under the canopy. Natalie rests her head on Nick's shoulder as he plays with her hair ... twirling and twisting it around his fingers.

He leans closer to her and whispers, "I am so proud of you."

"Thank you, Nicky. I can't go on by myself much longer, so once you're up to it, I expect you back."

"This is no time to be talking about work," Angie says to her daughter.

"Just making sure he doesn't disappear on us again. Personally, I don't think I can the handle the stress and neither can our mother. You understand, don't you Nick?"

"Perfectly," Nick replies as he continues to play with his sister's hair.

Gina helps her daughter into her robe and Ava climbs into Angie's lap. "Nicole is teaching me the backstroke."

"And how is that going?"

"Wonderfully. She's the perfect student," Nicole replies as she touches Ava's cute little nose. Nicole throughout glances across at Nick but he doesn't seem to acknowledge her attention.

"I have no doubt," Angie remarks. She turns to Nicole. "Do I detect a bit of a Kentucky accent?"

Nicole hesitates for a long, uncomfortable moment. "Most people don't catch that, but yes, I grew up there before moving to Vegas."

"Lovely country and wonderful people," Angie remarks.

"I guess that depends on the part of the state you visit. Where I'm from … well, it wasn't very pretty and the people weren't very wonderful."

"I'm sorry to hear that," Angie replies. "And were the people in Vegas any better?"

"No."

Angie reaches over and takes her hand. "Well, I can vouch for all the people present."

"I'm helping Nicole with her new computer," Ava says.

"What type of computer did you get?" Natalie asks.

"Your generous brother bought me the latest Mac."

"I accidently destroyed Nicole's computer," Nick remarks.

"How did you do that?" Natalie asks.

"It's a long story. I wouldn't want to stress you out with all the details," Nick replies and Natalie punches him in the arm.

"Don't be such an ass. And just for the record, I've been taking karate lessons."

"In your spare time?" Nick asks.

"Yes, it's amazing how much you can accomplish when you use your time efficiently. So you better not mess with me."

"I won't. Not even if you had a gun pointed at me and were ready to pull the trigger."

"Such a gentleman," Natalie remarks as she looks at Nicole and smiles.

"Oh, that I'm quite sure of … even though I think if I had a gun pointed at him, he might take some sort of action. Isn't that so, Nicky?"

"You're not my sister so I would recommend you never point a gun at me."

"What if I point a gun at you?" Ava asks as she climbs off Angie and crawls onto Nick's lap.

"And what would Chuck and Snoopy think about that?" Nick replies.

"They wouldn't like it," Ava whispers.

"I wouldn't think so," Nick remarks as he looks into her big, brown, curious eyes. "And who was the first president of the United States?"

"Washington."

"And the second, third, and fourth?"

"Adams, Jefferson, and Madison." she replies with little hesitancy.

"And the capitals of New York, California and Florida?"

"Albany, Sacramento and Tallahassee," she replies as Natalie reaches over and grabs her off Nick's lap.

Gina and Nick serve dinner on paper plates with plastic knives, forks and paper napkins.

"Hope I didn't overcook everything?" Frank asks as he sits down next to his wife.

Angie takes a bite of her steak. "It tastes absolutely wonderful."

"My husband has turned into a fabulous chef. Whoever would have thought … a tough guy from the Bronx. I don't even go into my kitchen anymore," she says as she winks at him.

Everyone helps clean up after dinner, then Nick and Ava leave to go watch the Charlie Brown marathon. Gina and Frank, confident their child is in safe hands, excuse themselves and go off to bed.

Angie turns to Nicole and remarks, "Those two really need some alone time."

"Gina's an amazing mother," Nicole replies.

Natalie, half asleep, turns to her mother. "I'm going to make an executive decision and give the crew the rest of the week off with pay. Can we stay here tonight and the next few days?"

"That sounds wonderful, sweetheart."

"Great! I'm going to join Nick and Ava." She kisses her mother and hugs Nicole. "Such a pleasure to meet you. See you tomorrow." Angie and Nicole sit alone by the pool.

Nicole turns to Angie. "How about we split a beer?"

Angie smiles. "I see my son has told you about some of my habits. Yes, that would be wonderful. It's such a beautiful night."

Nicole walks toward the house and can't help feeling that this was how it was meant to be … her and Angie, alone at the end of night, sharing a beer and maybe discovering some of each other's secrets. She feels like she did with Ava … an undeniable desire to be liked and loved by this captivating and intelligent person. A chill runs down her spine as she remembers Nick's warnings, but how could she be totally honest without alienating herself from these people?

The kitchen is dark, and when she opens the refrigerator, the light inside blinds her for a moment. *I must be crazy. Nick doesn't want to be with me. He's just feeling guilty for leaving his family and I'm the charity case that's making him feel better about himself.* She grabs a beer from the shelf and looks for cold glasses. She sets everything on the shiny granite counter and as the fridge closes, darkness sets in again. *Compared to these people, what am I? An unholy creature ... a dirty, disease-infected mosquito living in a swamp.* For some reason, her mind slips to Elizabeth, to the promise she made to the girl she loved ... the one hope at the end of a dark tunnel ... all that is left of that now is a pile of ashes in an urn in the back of her car. *I can't even set her free.*

She walks back outside carrying the beer and two chilled glasses. "Do you ever go back to Bronx?" she asks as she pours the beer.

"Occasionally, I still have some family and friends back there. We still own the house my children grew up in. My husband's family bought it for us as a wedding gift."

"Nick never talks about his father."

"He probably doesn't remember him. He was only two when his father was killed. Natalie had just turned one."

"My God, that sounds terrible."

"In exchange for the wedding gift, his family pressured my husband to get a *real* job. So he joined the police department, like his father and brothers, and two years after that, he was killed in the line of duty. It took me years before I ever talked to my in-laws again. They tried to give me money for the kids but I threw it back in their faces. My husband was a beautiful man. He wanted to be an artist, a painter, like Da Vinci or Picasso, and he had plenty of talent but his family was convinced he was just wasting his time on a stupid dream."

"That's so wrong. How did you manage?"

"The death benefits from the police department were enough to keep us going for a while, and the little he had in his pension plan helped. I got some modeling jobs, mostly local, and that was enough to keep us above water. Believe me, I couldn't afford to get my children the best of things but we were a lot better off than many families."

Angie takes a sip of beer. "Beer tastes so much better in a chilled glass."

"You did an amazing job raising your children. Your husband must be looking down and feeling awfully proud."

"I seriously hope so. At times when I look at my Nicky, I see my husband. He blessed me with the two greatest gifts in my life. He was the type of man they would have idolized … a father they would have easily looked up to. I still have all his paintings and sketches … many of them done on simple paper napkins."

Angie laughs as she takes another sip of beer. "I was his favorite subject."

"Of course you were. I imagine if you were alive during Da Vinci's time you would have been *his* favorite subject."

Angie reaches over and gently touches Nicole's face. "Personally, I think Mr. Da Vinci would have preferred you. You are so beautiful."

"Thank you. But I really don't think Mr. Da Vinci would have even noticed me if I were in the same room with you."

"Don't ever sell yourself short, sweetheart."

"Did you ever make up with your in-laws?"

"No, but eventually I allowed the children to visit them. I felt they had a right to know who their grandparents were on their father's side."

"And how did that go?"

"Honestly, I never asked and they never told me. I do know that whatever money they gave them went straight into the church's box for the poor. Natalie let that little secret slip out while we were visiting Nick in the hospital in Germany."

"It must have been torture for you when he was away."

"It was as though he stuck a dagger into our hearts. Someday, when I get up the courage, I'll ask him how he could do something like that to us. If it was to hurt me, well, he achieved his goal, but to hurt his sister is unimaginable to me. I cannot tell you how happy I was when she told me she was taking off the rest of week. She's been under so much pressure, and if Nick doesn't decide to come back soon I will see to it that the company is sold. I will not let any company undermine my daughter's health and well being."

"She seems to be a very strong person."

"She is. One does not achieve what she has without being strong, but when your partner ... your brother ... decides to go on a misguided adventure, it can break the strongest of people. They were inseparable. They collaborated on everything ... even though the idiots in this town assumed that Nick, being the guy, was the brains behind the operation. I guess if anything good came out of this affair it cleared up the misperception about my daughter. She can stand toe to toe with any guy, including her brother, and outshine all of them."

"Nick told me Natalie's brilliant and that she was finally getting the credit she deserved."

"Nick has always been her biggest fan and always refuted allegations that he was the genius behind everything. He always made sure that her name was the first to appear on all their productions, but stereotypes, especially in this town, are difficult to erase."

"I understand why you would be upset with Nick, but there's no denying that your son is a hero," Nicole says with conviction.

Angie looks directly at her "My son did what was expected of him. He should never have been in that situation in the first place."

"But he saved lives at the risk of losing his own. That's the definition of a hero."

Angie smiles. She takes Nicole by hand. "I want to show you something."

They walk down the hallway and open the door of the screening room. On the screen, like all the other times, are Charlie Brown, Snoopy and the Peanuts gang. Angie continues to hold Nicole's hand as they walk toward the center seats. Nick, Ava and Natalie sleep in three chairs that are reclined into beds, complete with pillows and blankets. Ava sleeps between the two adults with Natalie and Nick's arms wrapped around her.

"Those are the only three chairs that turn into beds. We had them built like that because at least one or two of us would always fall asleep while watching a movie. I don't know what I enjoyed more, the movies or being surrounded by my children. There was no better dream than waking up and seeing the faces of my two sleeping beauties."

"So there was a time when something else was on the screen besides Peanuts movies?"

"Yes. We have diverse tastes when it comes to movies, but now that Ava is here, it's Chuck and the gang all the time."

"Before Ava ever arrived, that's all that your son was looking at," Nicole remarks.

"Is that so," Angie replies as she takes one last long look at the sleeping trio. "I think it's time us ladies get some sleep too."

* *

In her room, Nicole takes off her robe and bathing suit and steps into the shower, turns on the water and allows it to splash against her body. She can't help but feel that she's entered an alternate universe, like in a comic book.

Somehow, she can't shake the feeling that Angie and Natalie know everything about her. Like Nick, they seem to have the power to look at a person and immediately know everything. The feeling is uncanny and weird. She thought that Nick was exaggerating about his mother, but if anything, he didn't tell half the story. She can still feel Angie's presence all around her: the penetrating eyes, the soothing touch, the enigmatic smile and the voice that could easily talk a suicidal person off a ledge.

After her shower, she sits on the bed in her pajamas and looks out the window at the swimming pool and the reflection of the palm trees on the surface of the water. She lays her head down on the pillow, pulls the blankets over her body and turns onto her side. If ever she wanted Nick to enter her room and just hold her, it was now.

Fifteen

When Nicole wakes up, Ava is looking down at her. She's dressed in her bathing suit and holding a breakfast tray filled with fresh biscuits, fruits, eggs, bacon, sausages and a glass of orange juice. The early morning sun rises through the branches of gently swaying trees and touches the backs of large, gaudy mansions.

"Wow, is that all for me?"

"Yes. Nick said you liked cold pizza for breakfast but we didn't have any..."

"Are you at least going to help me eat it?" Nicole asks as she sits up in bed and Ava sits beside her.

"I already ate breakfast. Cereal with milk," Ava replies with a tinge of sadness.

"Is that what you usually have?"

"Yes, but I used to have it with chocolate syrup. Even though everything came back cancer free they still don't want to take any chances. Yesterday was so much fun, but now it's back to healthy food all the time."

Nicole hides her smile. "That's because they love you so much."

"I know."

"Is everybody else up?"

"Mommy and Daddy are still asleep but Angie told me not to bug them. That it's good they were sleeping."

"Yes, sometimes getting a lot of sleep can work wonders."

"When are you and Nick getting married?"

"I don't think we're ever getting married. He didn't even look at me once last night," Nicole replies and immediately shivers at the words that just came out of her mouth.

"He's just trying to make up with Natalie. She's still very mad at him for going away." Ava leans toward her and lowers her voice. "I'm not suppose to talk about it, so please don't tell anybody … but I think he's a superhero, like Batman."

"Do you know where he went?"

"Of course. He went to fight the bad guys. I saw him in the hospital. It was very sad. So many soldiers were missing legs and hands."

"You went to Germany?"

"They didn't want to take me but I made them. They thought he was going to die but I knew he wouldn't. Superheroes don't die and once I got there, he got better."

"I can definitely see how you could have that effect on him."

"Angie and Natalie were there for a long time. All the sick soldiers were in love with them."

"I'm sure they must have fallen in love with you too."

"Yes, but I told them I was too young to get married. It made me very sad to have to say no, but I think they understood."

Nicole looks at Ava with amazement. "I'm sure they understood."

When Nicole finishes eating, she changes into her bathing suit and takes Ava's hand on their way down to the pool.

"Do you think your mother would get mad if I kidnapped you?" Nicole jokes.

"Yes. It would make her very sad and she would never stop crying and they would be the sad type of tears."

"How about if I kissed you a hundred times?"

Ava giggles and Nicole bends down and kisses her all over her face, ears and head.

"That wasn't a hundred," Ava remarks.

"Well, I don't want to use up all my kisses in one shot. It's still early."

They walk out the door to the pool. Nick sits at a table with Natalie at the far end of the pool. Papers are spread out across the table and they are talking quite seriously. Nicole looks across at them for a long moment. Ava looks up and pulls at Nicole's arm, "Don't worry, he's in love with you."

Nicole laughs as she looks down at the adorable child. "I guess if anyone would know it would be you."

"Yes, he tells me everything." They walk into the pool and Nicole asks, "How about we do a warm-up lap?" They swim slowly across the pool as Nicole keeps a vigilant eye on her pupil. They stop at the far end of the pool and rest on the edge, directly across from Nick and Natalie. "Good morning," Nicole says to them with a smile. Natalie looks across at them and calls out, "Good morning, ladies." Nick looks up from a piece of paper he is reading from and simply smiles at them. They swim back to the other side of the pool and begin their lesson. The early morning sun glistens off the water and illuminates the sprays of splashing water like pearls of heavenly magic accompanying the musical laugher of the child and her teacher.

Nick walks over to the side of the pool and looks happily across at Nicole as she lets go of Ava, and the child, like a champion, stays afloat on her back as she paddles with both arms. Nick claps, to the delight of Ava and Nicole.

"Can I speak to you for a moment?" Nick asks.

Nicole instructs Ava to continue practicing, then gets out of the pool and sits down with Nick at a separate table away from Natalie and where they can keep a close eye on the child.

"So, did you give my mother a foot massage last night?" Nick asks with a touch of sarcasm.

"I don't even know what that's suppose to mean."

"My mother couldn't stop talking about how wonderful she thinks you are. It's all she spoke about while we ate breakfast. If

I didn't know better, I'd swear she was speaking about one of her children … or about Ava."

"I sure hope you set her straight about me," Nicole remarks as she momentarily takes her eyes off Ava and looks at Nick.

"Actually, I agreed with everything she said."

"Really. I thought it wasn't a good idea to lie to your mother."

"I didn't lie to her. She simply detected the wonderful qualities in you that it took me a little longer to notice, but then we met under different circumstances."

"I stood up for you," Nicole remarks.

"I figured."

"It's time to come clean. Your mother and sister deserve answers."

"I wish I knew how."

"Why don't you follow the advice you gave me and simply be honest?"

Nicole reaches over and places her hand on top of his. They watch as Ava climbs out of the pool and runs into the arms of her adoring mother. "There really is no substitute."

"No, there really is no substitute," Nick agrees as he wiggles his fingers between Nicole's until their hands clasp together like an unbreakable chain.

Nick stands up, reaches over, and kisses Nicole on the mouth for a long and loving moment. "I'll see you in the house."

"Yeah, I'll see you in the house," Nicole remarks, her face suddenly glowing. With Nick out of earshot, she whispers to herself, "Wow! Maybe he does tell Ava everything."

Natalie walks toward Nicole, smiling and holding a folder filled with business papers, and sits down at the table.

"You look so happy," Natalie remarks.

"It's such a beautiful morning, it would be a crime to be anything but happy," Nicole says, then notices Natalie's huge smile. "And you, talk about looking happy, you look like you just got some great news."

"Is it that obvious? Yes, I'm thrilled. I just agreed to take off the whole month, instead of just a week. We're shutting down production, and Nick has promised to come back full time. We'll be a team like we have been nearly our entire lives."

"That's wonderful. Does that mean all is forgiven?" Nicole asks as though she's already privy to family secrets.

"Almost. He still has a few issues to resolve, but I have total trust in him. My brother is the best man I've ever known … he's quite resilient."

"Like a superhero."

"Ava?" Natalie asks with a knowing smile.

"Yes, Miss Ava. Maybe, one day she'll join your team."

"If that's what she wants … even though, in a very real way, she's already part of our team. I can't even begin to count how many ideas and observations have come out of her mouth that Nick and I use in our productions. Yesterday, when we got the news that her MRI came back clean and cancer free, I nearly peed my pants I was so happy."

"You could actually feel the tension leave Gina's body."

"Oh, I have no doubt … and I can't even begin to tell you how much she appreciated you going with her. Frank is wonderful, but his constant reassurances that everything is going to be okay have a tendency to stress Gina out even more."

"They're lucky to have you guys as friends."

"It works both ways. They've been there for us as much as we've been there for them. They're family."

"Doesn't it cause problems when you shut down production for a month."

"That's the beauty of being a totally independent company. No outside investors, one hundred percent family owned, and we put up all the money for our productions. The only thing we rely on the studios for is distribution, and we've made so much money for them that they are not going to utter a word, at least not to our faces. The crew will be getting paid for the month off, and since it doesn't interfere with any of the actors's schedules, it has all worked out perfectly."

"Wow! What an amazing business you guys have built."

"Our mommy taught us well."

Nicole momentarily lowers her gaze as a fickle display of sunshine reflects off the glass tabletop. She looks back up and gazes across at the unblemished, childlike complexion of the young lady sitting across from her. Natalie wears a simple, comfortable summer dress with a pair of flip-flops.

"Nick tells me that you're going to take custody of your younger sister and raise her on your own."

"That's the plan. The idea of her being raised by those disgusting, immoral excuses for human beings makes me cringe. In a year she will be a teenager, and once a girl starts maturing it is simply not safe. It's like open season and no hunting license is required."

"And your parents are just going to hand her over?"

"Happily. One less mouth to feed."

Natalie looks at her with a penetrating expression. Nicole buries the desire to lower her eyes and confronts Natalie's gaze with a similar intensity.

"Your sister is lucky to have you."

"I just can't stand by and see her future and life destroyed."

"And how about your future?"

"My future was decided a long time ago, without my consent. You grow up really quick where I come from."

"How old are you? Twenty-five, twenty-six, maybe twenty-seven at the most?"

"Does it matter?"

"I think so. If you plan on raising your sister correctly it's important that you lead by example. My mother was younger than you when my father was killed. A significant part of our education was watching our mother pursue her career goals with a passion and not only being the greatest mother but a participant in our lives."

"Your mother is a special person."

"So are you. It hasn't gone unnoticed how easily you've connected with Ava."

"Oh please, if kidnapping wasn't a crime I would kidnap her. Her laughter and her energy are just infectious..."

"And that's the way we all feel about her but—"

"She's so adorable, a pint-sized Einstein, and the way Gina tells it, you and your mother had a lot to do with that."

"Ava was born a genius. But we did work a lot with her when she was sick ... and I have no doubt that our persistence, patience and belief in her helped with her recovery. I know the situation is different with your sister, but in the end, they both deserve a future where they can shine ... but that doesn't mean that you should give up on your own dreams. Do you know where you plan on living once you take custody of her?"

"Not really, but the one thing I'm sure of is that it won't be Kentucky or Nevada."

"Well, that leaves forty-eight other states and the entire world," Natalie replies as Nicole laughs.

"You can live here," Natalie suggests. "God only knows this house is in desperate need of occupants. We're hoping that Gina and Frank decide to finally move out here, and if they knew that you and your sister were also going to be living here, that would make their decision so much easier. They wouldn't feel like they were imposing so much on our time, which they are definitely not doing, but it's hard to tell them that. And the Ava effect is miraculous. Just ask my brother."

"That's such a generous offer, and I am so touched, but—"

"Nick thinks you would make a wonderful film editor. My mother and I think that with a face like yours you should be in front of the camera, but we understand that past circumstances won't allow that, and we respect that."

Nicole looks down as the sun's reflection off the tabletop unmasks an unbearable shame. She looks as though she's been blindsided by a fifty-pound medicine ball. She feels her chest tighten as Natalie continues describing her possible future in the family business. "You would start off as an intern, and with the right amount of diligence and determination, we would expect you to move up the ladder quickly. Eventually you'd be making a very comfortable living. We'll help get your sister into a really good school and we'll take care of all expenses until you're soundly on your feet."

But Nicole doesn't hear a word of this. She is still stuck on Natalie's earlier words: *We understand that past circumstances won't allow that and we respect that.*

"Exactly, what has Nick told you about me?"

"That your favorite book is Hemingway's *The Sun Also Rises* and occasionally you use the name Catherine Barkley from *A Farewell to Arms.* You have wonderful taste in literature and that goes a very long way with my family."

"Thank you … and for the offer … excuse me…"

Nicole stands up, slips a robe over her swimsuit and heads into the house. She had been forced into a profession where taking off her clothes and having her body violated night after night was simply part of the job, but she'd never felt more bare and undressed … and now she would have to confront the source of her naked exposure.

Sixteen

"You son of a bitch."

Nick looks up from where he's sitting alone, watching Chuck, Snoopy and the gang. Before he can react, Nicole leans toward him and slaps him across the face, but it barely seems to register. He only sits up a little straighter and gently moves her to the side. "It's rude to block someone's view. I thought you knew better than that."

"What else did you tell them?"

"Only that your favorite novel is *The Sun Also Rises* and you enjoy using the pseudonym Catherine Barkley from *A Farewell to Arms*." He hesitates as he looks into her emotionally battered face. "And I told them that you were abused as a young teenage girl and forced to move to Vegas and coerced into working in a profession not of your choosing."

"So … you told them that I was a whore."

"I didn't use that word, and nor would I ever describe you that way."

"Does it matter?" Nicole is weeping and raging at the same time. "How could you? That was my story to tell, not yours."

"Did it stop Natalie from offering you a job and begging you to move into this house?"

"Are you so blind that you don't see the implications? At any moment the cops could knock on the door and arrest me."

"I would never let that happen. And for the record, you shot a dead guy in Las Vegas. I don't know what preceded the shot to the head but apparently he died of a heart attack. Didn't it seem a bit strange that there was no blood splatter after you shot him?"

"So that's the reason I couldn't wake the son of a bitch up and get the satisfaction of seeing him beg for his life. How did you find this out?"

"I read the autopsy report. Death by natural causes. Case closed."

"And what about Evan Thomas?"

"The FBI is convinced that the organization behind the prostitution ring had Evans killed. That a mob boss from Chicago named Costello ordered the hit. Couldn't risk a wacko druggie like Evans in the hands of the feds. Apparently, Evans was a charter member and helped get the whole operation started. When they started looking into his finances, they discovered an offshore account. The feds simply followed the money, linked it to Costello, discovered what they believe to be a prostitution ring recruiting underage girls and were a day or two away from arresting Evans when he met his untimely demise."

"And do the feds have a strong enough case against Costello to bring down the whole organization?"

"My guess is that we'll have the answer to that question very soon. So unless you have some other skeletons in your closet, I suggest that you concentrate on your sister and take advantage of the generous proposal my sister, mother and I have offered you."

"And what do you get out of all this?"

"Hopefully, a valuable addition to our family and our company. And maybe, an apology for the rude way you barged in here and assaulted me."

Nicole laughs. She flops down in her seat, flips off her sandals and puts her feet on Nick's lap. "A foot massage, please."

"Is that your way of saying you're sorry?"

"If that's what you want to believe, please go right ahead and believe it."

Nick starts massaging her feet. "And for the record, I did not mention your two greatest *hits* that we just discussed."

"I have no idea what you're talking about. You must have me confused with some other girl."

Nick smiles. "They would of found out about the rest of your history one way or another. That's why I told them. We do exhaustive background checks on all new employees. It doesn't matter if you're the greatest cameraperson or editor in the world. We need to protect everyone who works for us, and just because a person is great at their profession, it doesn't mean that they're not morally bankrupt."

"Did Miss Ava have to go through the same exhaustive background check?"

"No, she outsmarted us all."

"So if I take the job, do I report to Ava?"

"We all report to Ava."

Nicole laughs as she swings around in her seat and places her head on Nick's lap.

"I wasn't finished massaging your feet," Nick remarks as he runs his hand along the contours of her beautiful face.

"So back in the Bronx, some fifteen years ago, did you ever think you would fall in love with a girl from Appalachia?"

"And what makes you believe I'm in love with you?"

"A precocious little nine-year-old with amazing powers of observation told me," Nicole remarks with a sparkle in her eyes. "Should I tell her she's wrong?"

"No, that wouldn't be wise. And when did you realize you were in love with me?"

"When I realized you weren't lying about being super rich."

"So it was all about the money?"

"A girl has to look out for herself," Nicole replies.

But then she sits up and slides onto Nick's lap. She puts her arms around his neck and looks into his eyes. "The day you ripped the price tag off from around my neck. That's when I fell in love with you."

Seventeen

The following morning, Nicole hands Nick the keys to her car and he opens the trunk and puts their luggage inside. The arsenal of weapons has been removed.

"Hope you at least got a good price for all that hard-earned hardware."

"Yeah, peace of mind," Nick replies as he closes the trunk.

"Peace of mind doesn't pay the bills."

Nicole looks at the front door of the house. "I don't want to leave."

"We can skip Santa Barbara and simply stay another day."

She shakes her head.

"After we get back here with your sister, we can take a trip up to Santa Barbara."

"When we get back, you'll be lucky enough to have time to kiss me goodnight. Natalie isn't joking, and I fear her a lot more than I fear you."

"Go say goodbye to everyone and please don't even hint at the possibility that you might not come back."

"Aren't you coming?"

"I already said my goodbyes."

Nicole starts to walk toward the house but looks back, sighs deeply and smiles at Nick. She runs her hands through her dark, luminous hair and raises an eyebrow to the swanky southern California sunshine. Nick looks at her with an all-knowing expression as she enters the house, and for a moment, he is reminded of one of the first times he spoke to her. *You're not one to forget? ... Nor do I forgive.* The makeover of Nicole was far from complete.

Nick was cognizant as he watched Nicole pass through the doors of the house and into the hands of his loving family that she knew the difference between right and wrong ... between love and betrayal. She knew these things as well as anyone in his family, and that was what left him with lingering doubts about her motives and plans. As he listened to the laughter and cries inside the house, he shook with the understanding that Nicole, like Natalie, Angie, Gina and Frank, would react to an injustice against a loved one with overwhelming retaliation. Their methods might differ, but they would not rest until the punishment was complete, and Nick sensed that the punishment Nicole intended to mete out to those who took Elizabeth away from her was not finished.

Nick opens the front door of the car and tucks his Maxim 9 under the seat. He reaches into a satchel for a manila envelope and slides out a photo. It's Anthony Mancuso, the man in the Armani suit. Below the image a caption reads: *Wanted for three murders, extortion, and soliciting underage girls into prostitution. Considered extremely dangerous and loyal to Costello.*

Nicole walks out of the house holding Ava's hand, and Nick quickly replaces the photo into the envelope and slides it into the satchel. Ava looks at Nicole intently and reveals her latest precocious move. She remarks, "I've set up a separate email for you so there is never a reason not to keep in touch."

"Thank you, sweetheart. I love you so much." Nicole hugs Ava and holds onto the child as though she is a nugget of gold. She gives her a last kiss, and then Ava goes to Nick, hugs and kisses him, and with tears in her eyes, she runs into the house. Nick hands Nicole the keys to the car and surprisingly, she hands them back.

He drives out of the entrance to the house, makes a right on Sunset Boulevard and drives west toward the beach. Nicole gazes out the window.

"It's okay to cry, Nicole. I won't think of you as any less dangerous."

She turns and hits him in the arm. "You're a real asshole."

"Now, now ... where is all that warmth and love you showered me with just yesterday in the screening room?"

"I take it all back, and for the record I've regretted it ever since."

"Reverting back to the schoolyard?" Nick asks.

"Yes! After all, I was denied ever being a teenager ... or have you forgotten that? My God, it must have been so difficult for you to grow up surrounded by two such beautiful women with superior intellect and class. You must have felt invisible."

"Add you, Gina and Ava to the mix and I really feel invisible, but I must admit the scenery just keeps getting better."

Nicole shakes her head. "And another thing, this mean-hearted bitch never did hear you say *I love you* during that moment we had yesterday."

"If you have any doubt about that, you're not nearly as smart as I give you credit for."

"I have no doubt about it, but it would have been nice to hear it."

"I love you, Nicole."

"Nice try, asshole," Nicole replies as her phone beeps. She slides the screen over and reads an email from Ava. *Miss you a bunch. Love you so much. Please give your future husband a kiss from me.*

"From Ava?" Nick asks.

"Yes."

"Expect about twenty emails a day from her."

"Great! I wish it were a hundred. Whatever she has to say has to be a lot more interesting than listening to you."

"Whatever, lovelymermaid101." He grins. "Ava told me the email address she chose for you. She also reminded me to tell you how much I love you at least ten times a day."

"Well, you're way behind."

"It's early."

Nicole reaches over and kisses Nick on the cheek. "A request from Miss Ava. And by the way, did you straighten everything out with your mother, or am I not supposed to ask about that?"

"No, you can ask, and *yes* I did straighten everything out."

"That's great! Hopefully, you didn't tell her that load of bullshit about searching for a higher purpose."

"I told her I was truly sorry for the pain I caused her and Natalie. That I regretted it almost from the moment I signed on the dotted line but was too proud to turn back. In a blissful moment of immaturity, I actually believed that I was a *superhero* like the ones I created numerous times in the movies we made. Ironic, since the price I paid was nothing compared to the pain and suffering I caused the two people in the world I love and cherish the most."

"They've forgiven you. That I'm sure of."

"Yes, it's in their nature, but I don't know if I can ever forgive myself. Even after living through the agony I saw on my mother's face every time she looked at a picture of my father, I went off and had her suffer a more prolonged pain and, once again, ask her herself a question she has never stopped asking since my father was killed ... *what did I do wrong?*"

"She told me it was her in-laws who forced your father to join the police force."

"Yes, and that's the truth. But before he made that fateful decision they had talked about moving far away, leaving them the house, and escaping their orbit of influence and the constant nagging. She begged, but with two toddlers he talked her out of it. The expenses would be too much and he couldn't risk, or fathom the possibility, that he wouldn't be able to provide for her and the children."

"And so all these years she has blamed herself for not begging enough ..."

"And I compounded her grief a million times over because my actions defied logic and not only did I hurt her but betrayed my sister."

Eighteen

Nick looks out the window of their hotel room at the beautiful city of Santa Barbara. The contrast between this beachside paradise and where he was less than six months ago could not be more striking. The stench of death, the cries of the soldiers and the sterile atmosphere of the hospital were so vivid that it was like he was experiencing a sensory overload and was about to explode, but he would never let that happen. Like so many other things, he had no other option but to bury the last two years as much as was possible. It was when he closed his eyes and slept that he couldn't control the narrative. It was like the rough cut of a horror movie before the editor turns it into something meaningful.

Nicole steps out of the bathroom in a lovely white summer dress and looks across at Nick staring out the window.

"A penny for your thoughts," she says in a soothing and playful manner.

"A penny … that's kind of cheap."

"I would pay a lot more if I thought that would allow me a few more glimpses into the mind of Nicholas Righetti."

"You would be greatly disappointed and I wouldn't want you to waste your money."

"Why don't you let me decide that," Nicole remarks as Nick turns and looks at his beautiful lady.

"What's wrong … you don't like?" Nicole asks as she twirls around and lifts her dress slightly above her knees.

"There's not a single thing not to love." He takes her hand and they walk down to the edge of the ocean.

Nicole slips off her sandals and steps into the water. She splashes Nick with her foot and is laughing and moving backwards when a wave strikes her from the back and knocks her down. With a little shriek of surprise she steadies herself and stands up, her summer dress soaked. Silhouetted against the majestic Pacific Ocean, the golden rays of the sun strike the lovely lady as a divine halo arises from the ocean spray and casts a warm glow across her perfectly defined figure.

Nick grabs her by the waist and pulls her close. She giggles as he runs his hands through her hair. They look into each other's eyes, two unsettled souls connected by the solace and protection they provide each other. They kiss passionately for a long time.

Nicole runs back into the water, spins around, and throws her hands up to the sky. "It's so beautiful, here. So beautiful!"

* *

Nicole and Nick sit at a window table with an ocean view at the famous Harbor Restaurant on Stearns Wharf in Santa Barbara. They eat fresh oysters and clams and drink Cristal Champagne. Nicole occasionally looks out at the ocean as though hypnotized.

"Nope. Never stepped foot in an ocean until today."

"Didn't you touch the ocean even once on the night I destroyed your computer?" Nick asks.

"Don't have a clue what you're talking about. You must be thinking of another girl."

"Certainly don't remember that other girl wearing a summer dress. You're probably right. I must be mistaken."

"Your sister looked so comfortable wearing this type of dress. I told her that I just had to get some and a few hours later she had a whole box delivered to me. She's such a doll."

Nicole turns and looks across at the bar. The man in the Armani suit, Anthony Mancuso, stands there and slowly sips his drink. He looks around as though he is waiting for someone.

"I know that guy," Nicole says, her face reddening.

Nick looks over. "From Vegas?"

"Yeah, and no, he wasn't a client. At first I thought he worked for that piece-of-shit Evans, but then I realized that he works for the company. He's a hitman." She looks back at Nick. "And I'm the target."

"Maybe he's just here having a drink."

"I don't believe in coincidence and I know damn well you don't."

"Finish your food as though you don't suspect anything. I'll pay. On our way out make sure he gets a good look at you … a really good look."

"I'm not carrying … This could turn into a suicide."

"Trust me."

Nick pays the bill and they walk toward the bar. Nicole looks directly at Anthony Mancuso and a spark of recognition registers in both their eyes. Once outside, Nick takes Nicole by the arm and leads her toward the edge of the wharf, about thirty feet from the entrance of the restaurant.

"And is this your plan … to sit here and let him come out and gun us both down?"

"He's not reckless. He's calculating and he knows the feds are all over the place. Costello is lucky if he survives the rest of the week."

Nick reaches behind his back and takes out the Maxim 9 he has hidden beneath his sports coat. He places the gun between his legs and crosses his right leg over his left to provide cover.

"No," Nicole says. "This is my fight. Give me the gun. I'll take care of this son of a bitch."

"What are you going to do, just gun him down? If he were here to kill you, he would have followed us out of the bar. When he comes out, go back in the restaurant, sit at the bar and order a drink. And don't move from there until I come back. I promise, I'm just going to follow him to see where he goes."

"You promise, no heroics?"

"I promise."

One hour later, Anthony Mancuso walks out of the restaurant and in the opposite direction of where Nick and Nicole sit watching. Nicole gets up and goes back into the restaurant while Nick trails Anthony through a maze of people, staying about fifty feet behind. The squawking of seagulls pierces the air above. In the distance, the sun settles into the ocean. As they approach the entrance to the wharf, Nick picks up his pace and moves closer to him.

Anthony turns left, onto the main boulevard running along the beach, and suddenly Nick is there with his gun out and the barrel shoved into the lower part of Anthony's spine.

"Don't even think about turning around because if you do I will send a bullet straight up your spine and by the time they get you to the hospital and save your life, you'll wish you were dead. Lovely night, isn't it Anthony? Just keep on walking."

"What do you want?"

"What every boy from the Bronx wants … to play center field for the New York Yankees. Now, see those benches? Walk over there, take off your jacket, very slowly, and lay it on the last bench."

Anthony starts to move forward and Nick follows closely behind with the gun pointed directly at him.

"By the way, you have wonderful taste in clothes. What's Costello paying a guy like you these days?"

Anthony looks out at the people on the beach as he slips off his jacket and sets it on the bench.

"Now, bend down and pull up your trousers and take out the gun you have strapped around your ankle."

Anthony takes out his gun and puts it on top of his jacket.

"Empty your front pockets, keep your wallet and hand me your car keys. And remember, one wrong move and a hospital bed is in your near future."

They start walking again. "So tell me, who's your target here in beautiful Santa Barbara?"

"There is no target."

"Really, not a pretty brunette with a killer body forced into prostitution by you and your boss?"

"I have no idea what you're talking about. I'm not here to kill anyone. Like everyone else in the company, I'm on the run ... trying to get as far away from Costello as possible."

"Did you kill Evan Thomas?"

"No, someone beat me to the job, but how I would've loved to have erased that fungus from this earth. Sadly, someone else got to wipe the world clean of that son of a bitch."

"Now is that anyway to talk about the dead?"

"Who are you working for?"

"Costello."

"Bullshit. He would never turn on me."

"Please, Anthony. So naïve, after all this time. You're the guy who knows everything from the start. You're the one person who can tie him to the entire operation. He has twenty bodyguards protecting him. Surely, you understand how a paranoid mind operates."

They stop in front of a BMW and Nick hits a button on the key chain and the trunk opens. "I hear these cars last forever ... but then any wise man knows that nothing lasts forever. Get in!"

"No!"

"Fine, have it your way."

Anthony spins around and is treated to a devastating kick to the midsection that sends him flying into the trunk. Nick punches him across the face, knocking him out. He closes the trunk and locks it.

"Told you not to turn around, you piece of shit." He slams the car keys on the top of the trunk. "Eventually, we all pay for our sins." He walks away.

Nineteen

Nick watches from a distance as FBI, local police and SWAT teams surround the BMW. They open the trunk and pull Anthony Mancuso out, then handcuff him and put him in the back seat of a police car.

Nick pulls out his phone and calls Nicole. "I should be there in a few minutes. Please order me a chocolate dessert and a couple of cold beers. The man in the Armani suit should be the lead story on tonight's news."

Nicole relaxes visibly as soon as Nick enters the restaurant. She can barely suppress the enormous smile that's spreading across her face, but she forces herself to frown as Nick joins her and sits across from her at a table overlooking the ocean. In the middle of the table sits a chocolate mousse pie. Nicole drinks a mojito as she samples the pastry and a little bit of the chocolate.

"Tastes good?"

"Delicious!"

Nick grabs a frosty beer out of a bucket filled with ice.

"So, what happened to the man in the Armani suit?"

"He decided to take a nap in the trunk of his car just as the FBI and SWAT teams showed up. But a few minutes before that, we had a very civil conversation. You weren't a target. He had no idea who you were. He came up from Los Angeles trying to keep ahead of the feds. He was supposed to take out Thomas but someone beat him to it."

"And you believe him?"

"Yes. The people involved in the operation are on the run. I imagine Costello's days are numbered."

Nicole shakes her head, then leans across the table and slaps Nick across the face.

"Okay … that's the second time in two days."

"Just be happy I don't kick your ass from one end of this restaurant to the next. You stupid, inconsiderate ass. No heroics, you promised! What would I say to your family if, God forbid, you got yourself killed trying to save a whore like me. Tell me, Nick, how would I explain that?"

"It didn't happen, so why don't you calm down. And I told you not to use that word."

"I'll use it if I want to, and I'll calm down once you're out of my life for good."

"You don't mean that."

"Yes, I do. I'm sorry, but that's just the way it has to be."

"What's the real reason we're in Santa Barbara?"

"Because it's where I am going to spread Elizabeth's ashes."

She looks out the window at the ocean and starts to cry. "We always talked about coming here once we were free. Neither of us had ever seen the ocean and the pictures always made it look so pretty and clean. That's why I'm here."

Nick looks at her, then lowers his eyes and shakes his head. The missing piece from the puzzle. A farewell to a loved one who was way too good for this world.

Twenty

Nick sits on the bed in the hotel room waiting for Nicole to come out of the bathroom. She opens the door and sits down next to him.

Nick takes her hand. "When Natalie and I didn't feel comfortable going to our mom with a problem, we would often go visit our father's grave. Even though neither of us remember him, when we kneeled down beside his grave we would come up with an answer to our problem. It was a great comfort just knowing he was there and we could visit him whenever we wanted. I guess what I'm trying to say is that before you set free Elizabeth's ashes over the ocean, you might want to reconsider."

"It's not like my memories of her are going anywhere."

Nicole stretches out next to him and shuts off the lamp beside the bed. Nick leans over her and whispers, "I love you so much, Nicole."

"I know you do and I love you so much. And no, I'm not running away, but I'm also not ready to forgive you for your inane heroics. And just for the record you're still six *I love you's* away from the targeted amount set by Miss Ava."

"And it would be a sin to disobey her."

Yes, it would be. But I'll tell you what, if you whisper one more time in my ear how much you love me and hold me tight all night long I won't tell."

Nick does as he's asked and tries not to move or burst into a million pieces.

* *

Nick wakes up as Nicole stirs. She looks down at him with her beautiful and mesmerizing eyes. "I would love to get an early start, if that's okay with you."

"Sounds great," Nick replies as Nicole starts to get up from the bed. "And Elizabeth's ashes?"

"You were right, I can't part with them. She's just going to have to go on whatever ride life takes me on."

Nick drives out of the parking lot of the hotel and onto the main road that leads to US 101. Nicole lowers the window and breathes in the ocean air. "It's so lovely and clean. Don't forget your promise — when Natalie finally gives us a vacation you are going to take me back to this heavenly paradise."

"You can count on that," Nick replies.

"Really, your promises haven't meant much lately," Nicole remarks as she takes her phone out of her purse and looks down at all the emails left by Ava throughout the night. "Does Gina know that her lovely daughter is up half the night writing emails?"

"I'm sure she does, but what's she supposed to do? The child has an abundance of energy and by the time Gina closes her eyes at night she's completely exhausted."

"If I didn't know better, I would think she's your child. You both have an aversion to sleeping."

"I slept wonderfully last night."

"Of course you did. You had me to hold on to," Nicole remarks with a laugh as she reaches over and kisses Nick on the cheek a bunch of times. "Just following orders from Miss Ava. For all we know, she might be listening in. And by the way, Speed Racer, I'll take over the driving once I finish replying to all my emails. I'd love to get to our destination before we turn fifty."

* *

Nicole pulls into a hotel parking lot in Albuquerque, New Mexico. She parks and they walk into the hotel. It's late and the sky is littered with stars and an eerie sense of nothingness. They stop at the hotel bar and sit down. Nick orders a beer and Nicole a white wine.

"You see, if I let *you* drive, we might still be in California. Instead, we're nearly halfway there. So it really is true that New Yorkers can't drive, or is it just boys from the Bronx?"

"I think it's a little bit of both," Nick replies and laughs.

Nicole glances up at the TV and asks the bartender if he could make it louder.

In a stunning string of events, the FBI, along with other federal and local law enforcement, have announced that they have uncovered a human trafficking operation, originating in the Appalachia regions of Georgia, Alabama and Kentucky. Girls no older than fifteen, sold by parents, guardians and relatives into a life of prostitution. Before entering the profession as high-end prostitutes, the girls are schooled in an old monastery on the banks of the Hudson River in upstate New York.

The monastery, with Latin inscriptions of holy verses engraved in the masonry, is shown on the TV. Other footage shows police officers leading doctors, educators, politicians and Ms. Lynch, the hall monitor with the soft and soothing touch, out of the buildings and into police vans.

The head of the operation, reputed mob figure Carmine Costello, recruited investors throughout the world of entertainment, Wall Street and Fortune-500 companies to start the illegal business, which the FBI estimated has earned a net profit of half a billion dollars a year. In a shocking development today, Mr. Costello met an untimely death as he got into his automobile surrounded by bodyguards. We would like to caution our viewers that this next piece of eyewitness tape is graphic and that some may find it disturbing to watch.

Shaky video footage shows Carmine Costello and his associates getting into his car and a few moments later, the car exploding into a million pieces.

A spokesperson for the FBI said the death of Mr. Costello and his associates was under investigation. In another related event, Anthony Mancuso, reputed hitman and enforcer for the Costello Family, was shot to death as he tried to escape while being handed over to the FBI from the local police in Santa Barbara, California. And as if this story couldn't get any more bizarre, the Las Vegas leaders of this high-end prostitution ring refused to surrender to law enforcement and instead entered into a gun fight with the FBI and SWAT teams. All five members of the ring were killed, while eyewitness reports suggest that many of the girls forced into prostitution looked on and cheered.

Images of five bodies covered in black canvas are shown on the TV. The faces of several girls standing nearby are blacked out.

As the newscaster moves on to an unrelated story, Nicole looks at Nick. "It's even hard for *me* to believe just how far your reach extends."

She gets up and walks away as Nick pays the bartender who remarks, "Can you believe this type of shit takes place in this country?"

Nick shakes his head and gets into the elevator with Nicole. "I had very little to do with any of this," he says to a disbelieving Nicole.

"Of course not! What, did you have Frank provide them with all the information?"

"I would never get Frank involved with any of this, especially not with Ava and Gina to take care of."

"So … what, did you outsource the story?"

"I simply made sure that neither you nor I would ever be involved. You're free, Nicole."

"Strange, I thought if anyone would understand it would be you. I could never be free. I'll always be a prisoner."

Twenty-One

Back in their hotel room, Nicole opens the minibar, takes out a bottle of bourbon and hands Nick a beer. She pours the bourbon into a glass and remarks, "At first, you made me feel no different than the whore … I mean, sex slave, I was for the last seven years … paying for everything, handing me ten thousand dollars like it was nothing. The only difference was that you didn't ask for anything in return … at least not physically."

She sits down on the bed, arranges a number of pillows behind her and leans back as she sips her drink. "Wow … never have I been so wrong about a person."

"What's your point?"

She shakes her head. "I really don't know. Why don't you help me out? After all, that's what you do best … you help people … you save people … even when it puts you in danger."

She takes another sip of her drink. "When do I get to do something for you? Surely, there has to be some type of reward you're expecting at the end of all this?"

"I've already received my reward, and in many ways it exceeded all expectations."

"Please, stop talking in riddles. Surely, your reward can't be saving the hooker with the heart of gold who's in distress. That's a story that's been written and rewritten too many times and only takes place in the make-believe world of books and movies. The make-believe world that has caused your family so much pain and grief." Nicole's speech is interrupted by a long string of email alerts on her phone.

"Why don't you look at your emails? You might find the answer to your question in the uncensored comments of your little friend. And later when you look into the mirror, look really close, and for once try not to see a whore in distress."

Nicole finishes her drink, reaches into her purse, and takes out her phone to review the day's emails from Ava. The little genius has outdone herself; Nicole's inbox is filled with newsy notes about life at home, a funny, made-up story about Nicole's future wedding to Nick, with Snoopy and the gang serving as their attendants, a Charlie Brown meme, and one email filled with nothing but hearts. Nicole laughs and shakes her head as she marvels at the strength of her attachment to this precocious little girl who is constantly forgetting about her own struggles and making others happy. It strikes her that Ava has already begun to feel more like a daughter than the daughter of new friends.

Later, when Nicole stares into the bathroom mirror, she sees for the first time the person she has evolved into since she met Nick. The beautiful lady energized by the people who have entered her life and bestowed upon her an unconditional love and respect that she had only experienced with Elizabeth. Yes, the shackles have been removed, and it's time to spread her wings and squawk happily like a seagull and enjoy her newfound freedom. She changes into her Bugs Bunny pajamas, opens the bathroom door, and pirouettes like a ballerina and kneels down before Nick who lies on the couch. "Would the handsome gentleman be so kind as to dance with the lady?" Nick chortles and shoots her a look like she's the biggest, sweetest dork in the world, but stands up and replies, "I would be honored."

They're laughing and dancing as Nick turns her round and round, dexterously maneuvering her around the furniture and finally into her arms. "And do you approve of the attire?"

"Bugs has never looked better."

"Thank you, sir."

"And would the lovely lady give me the honor of marrying her?"

Nicole catches her breath and almost falls out of step, then recovers.

"The lady would love nothing better, but has the handsome gentlemen thought of the consequences? My past could pop up anywhere, in the supermarket, in a restaurant…" Nick rests a finger against her lips and replies, "Yes, and the gentleman is unconcerned *with silly whims and fancies frantic.*" Tears well up in Nicole's eyes as they dance cheek to cheek. "And what about the beautiful lady? Can she live with my limitations?" Nicole puts a finger to his mouth and says, "The lady only requires a loving kiss before we go to sleep and for the gentleman to hold her lovingly throughout the night."

"And does that mean a *yes* to my proposal?"

"Yes, yes, yes." She throws her arms around Nick and they kiss passionately.

* *

Nick holds Nicole as he affectionately caresses her hair while admiring her Bugs Bunny pajamas.

"Would tomorrow be too early for you?"

"You want to get married tomorrow?"

"Yes. In Independence, Missouri, at the Little Brown Church not far from the home of President Truman."

"Is President Truman one of your heroes?"

"Yes."

She turns and looks up at him and smiles. "At times you are so predictable. Of course he's one of your heroes. Besides President Lincoln, no president has been so generous toward a defeated enemy."

"You're so much more than just a beautiful, breathtaking, and stunning lady."

"Thank you. And how about your mother and sister, and Ava? They might not be so happy about us eloping."

"They'll be the most happy. Just give them a call and tell them. If they sound even a little unhappy, we can wait until we get back."

"I need to know … why so quickly?"

"Besides being madly in love with you, I want your sister to have no doubts that she is entering into a union that is strong, united and filled with love and support for her."

Nicole smiles. "Well, I don't know about you, but I'm way too excited to go to sleep. And if we plan on getting married in Independence, Missouri tomorrow, I think we should get on the road, like, right now."

Nick reaches down, looks deep into her eyes and kisses her sweet mouth until they forget where they are.

Twenty-Two

Nick sits in the passenger seat of the car and watches Nicole walk toward him with her cell phone in hand and a huge smile on her face.

"And how did it go?" he asks when she gets in the car.

"They were so excited and happy, and all Ava could tell me was 'I told you, I told you he was in love with you.' I'm supposed to take as many pictures as humanly possible and to immediately email them to her. Also, she told me to kiss you a hundred times but we don't have time for that so this will just have to do for now..." She reaches over and kisses him.

Nicole starts the car, turns on the radio and the Rascals "How Can I be Sure" comes on. She starts to sing to the song as Nick looks at her and thinks that this is the first time he could say with certainty that she was truly and undeniably happy.

Twelve hours later, after driving the whole night and most of the morning, they enter Independence, Missouri. They stop at the President's house where he and his wife Bess lived during their whole, long marriage ... except when Mr. Truman served in the Senate, as Vice President, and during his term as President in the White House.

The house, which has been turned into a museum, is closed, but Nick takes Nicole by the hand and they walk around the entire property, marveling at its small size. Nick points out that the Truman home is smaller than the house that he, Natalie, and their mom lived in in the Bronx. Before getting into their car, Nick stops before a large oak tree beside the house and places his hand on it for a long moment. "Leaving the house to go on his long strolls he would always touch this tree and say, *keep up the good work.*"

Nicole parks in front of the Little Brown Church and turns to Nick and says, "Last chance to come to your senses."

"Not a chance, but I'm embarrassed to say that I don't have a ring for you … once the ceremony is over that'll be the first thing we do."

Nicole reaches into her purse and takes out a simple gold ring with an inscription engraved in the interior: *Love always, Nicole and Elizabeth.* She hands it to Nick and asks, "Would you mind if I use this as my wedding ring, forever and forever? It would mean more to me than all the diamonds in the world."

"I would be honored," Nick replies as he takes off the only ring on his fingers and hands it to Nicole. "This was my father's."

"It's perfect."

They get out of the car and walk into the church. Apart from the preacher and an organist who serves also as a witness, the building is empty. After they introduce themselves and are led to their positions, the preacher starts the ceremony. When he comes to the exchange of rings he asks, "And have you prepared vows?" Nicole and Nick look at each other, confused, and then Nicole says, "I have something I would like to say and I am fairly certain that my soon-to-be husband will be able to join in. Nicole looks directly at Nick and recites the lines from Byron's poem,

Our love is fix'd, I think we've proved it;
Nor time, nor place, nor art have mov'd it;
Then wherefore should we sigh and whine,

Nicole stops and Nick continues,

With groundless jealousy repine;
With silly whims, and fancies frantic,
Merely to make our love romantic?
Our love is fix'd, I think we've proved it;
Nor time, nor place, nor art have mov'd it

They exchange rings and the preacher pronounces them husband and wife.

* *

The next day, Nick steps out of a limousine that Nicole parks at the peak of a hill — a limousine not much different than the one Madam Johnson took little Nicole away in. He takes a briefcase from the limo and walks down the hill where an old man and a young teenage girl sit on a rickety wooden bench. Nicole, who is behind the wheel of the car, watches her husband walk toward them. They had agreed that they wanted this arrangement to proceed just as the previous one had. It nauseated both of them to hand the money over, but they didn't want to cause any problems that could jeopardize the operation. Finally, Nicole's promise to her sister would be fulfilled and hopefully the feds would shut down this operation once and for all.

At the bottom of the hill, Nick approaches the bench and glares down at the old man, then hands him the briefcase. The old man opens it, looks at the stacks of money inside and nods his head. He closes it, and takes the papers Nick is holding out to him, signs them and hands them back.

"Go with the man," he mutters to the girl next to him, waving his hand toward Nick. He doesn't look at her. He's already opening the briefcase again, his eyes brightening. Nick takes the girl's hand and a small, beat-up suitcase, and walks back toward the limousine.

"Don't be afraid. I have a really nice surprise for you," Nick says as they walk up the hill. He opens the front passenger door of the limo and motions for the girl to climb in. As soon as she does, Nicole, behind the wheel of the car, reaches across the seat and grabs her sister, and hugs and kisses her. "I promised I would come back for you. I promised."

Caroline, after a little hesitation, says, "Nicole! Nicole, is it really you?"

"Yes, sweetheart, it's really me. Oh my God, I have waited so long, so long. I love you so much."

Nick buckles the youngster in and sits in the back. Nicole drives away as Nick looks at the two girls up front. He muses at how much they look alike. Looking into Caroline's face was like looking at a younger version of Nicole.

Nick turns the limousine in at the rental shop as he looks across at Nicole fussing over Caroline ... fixing her hair, straightening out her clothes and kissing and hugging her. Nick thinks back to the first time they met in Vegas. The confident, stylish, mysterious lady ordering mojitos did not seem to exist anymore ... only her loveliness ... and a spiritual reawakening of a lost soul.

Nick joins the ladies and Nicole remarks, "You know, handsome and courageous husband, that limo was quite comfortable and I would hate to think that Caroline will have to sit all crumpled up in the backseat of my car all way back to Los Angeles."

"Are you sure you're the same girl who couldn't wait to get behind the wheel of my mother's Ferrari?"

"Oh, I'm still that girl, but circumstances have changed and it's not like the Ferrari won't still be there when we get back."

They get into Nicole's car and drive to a dealership.

Twenty-Three

Nicole tearfully waves goodbye as her car is driven away. "Why are you crying, Nicole? Is it because of me?" Caroline asks, but Nicole quickly reassures her. "No! No! My sweet angel, when I look at you the only tears I shed are happy ones. I love you so much." She hugs Caroline as Nick hands her the keys to a red Chevrolet Suburban truck. They get in and Nicole stretches her arms and legs.

"Wow! This feels more like a house." She looks back at Caroline. "You have enough room back there, sweetie?"

Caroline looks around as though lost in a beautiful dream and nods. "It's bigger than my bed back home."

Nicole grabs Nick's hand and kisses it over and over again. "Thank you. Thank you." Nicole drives off and parks in the parking lot of a high-end steakhouse.

* *

Inside the restaurant, Caroline lifts her elbows off the dark wood table as she digs into the bottom of a tall chocolate sundae. As a waitress starts to clear their plates, the girl asks Nicole if she can use the bathroom.

"I'll show her where the bathrooms are … just down the hall," the server offers kindly. She escorts Caroline to the restrooms as Nicole watches them with a worried look on her face.

"Maybe I should go with her?"

"She'll be fine," Nick reassures her as he gently takes her hand. "She's your daughter, isn't she?"

Nicole, taken aback, remains silent for a long moment and then replies, "Yes. Does that make a difference?"

"Not one bit."

"She's perfectly normal."

"I have no doubt. A little shy, but after a couple of days with you, that shouldn't be a problem."

"Do you really think it will take that long?"

"Probably not."

She leans back against Nick and looks up at him. Her face goes paler than Nick has ever seen it as she forces the words out. "I was raped ... by my uncle ... on my thirteen birthday. He said it was his present to me, and naturally I, always being ahead of the curve, got pregnant. When my parents found out, they pulled me out of school and my mother pretended to be pregnant the whole time, using pillows as a disguise. I gave birth in the trailer we lived in with the help of the town's only doctor, a drunken GP. I was told in no uncertain terms that I was not the mother of the child. I was not even allowed to feed the baby. I was scared and said nothing." She suddenly stops, sighs, and wipes tears from her eyes.

"I recovered quickly from the pregnancy and within three months I was back at school looking as trim and fit and, well, as beautiful as ever. When Madam Johnson and her group of perverts started scouting for recruits they had no idea I had already given birth to a child. Caroline was nearly two by then and everyone just assumed she was my baby sister. When I found myself in the limousine with Madam Johnson and she did her examination she immediately was able to tell I had given birth. She asked, but even then I was too scared to tell the truth, and so I said nothing. She simply remarked that I was *too beautiful to pass up* and that I would *be the exception.* You must promise me Nicky that you will never tell anyone. Caroline has no idea, and it would destroy her."

"Of course," Nick promises quickly. "I promise, this will always remain between my wife and her husband."

And she leans further back into the safety of his arms.

Epilogue

Two days later, they arrived back in Los Angeles and were greeted with an abundance of love, hugs and kisses, and constant reminders from Natalie that in just a few more weeks, her brother would be going back to work with her. Once again they would be a team, but with a wonderful addition to the lineup.

There was such joy on his mother's face and happiness in his sister's smile that Nick finally felt that the suffering and agony he'd caused both of them was now in the past.

The cold and empty house that Nick first brought Nicole into was now filled with the laughter of children and the gaiety of a large and extended family. Gina and Frank and of course, Ava, had decided that they were moving permanently to Los Angeles and would be living in the house … not that they had a choice. Ava insisted that they live there and the matter was settled without further discussion.

Ava and Caroline, despite the age difference, became great friends, akin to sisters. Under the tutelage of Miss Ava, Angie, Natalie, Nick and Nicole, Caroline blossomed into a studious and creative child … thirsty for knowledge.

In an ironic twist of fate, at the same time that Nicole placed Elizabeth's urn on the mantle in the bedroom she shared with Nick, the Los Angeles Coroner's Office cremated the remains of Evan Thomas and Anthony Mancuso and placed their ashes in metal cans and put them on a shelf with other unclaimed remains. The family of Evan Thomas declined to claim the remains. As for Anthony Mancuso, he had no relatives or friends. They were all blown up in an unsolved car explosion back in Chicago.

Nicole, to no one's surprise, excelled as an apprentice editor and quickly moved up the ladder to become an assistant editor and finally head editor. Natalie and Nick were so impressed that she was given a vote on all matters related to the company, including properties it was interested in acquiring, such as books and screenplays.

Nick made it perfectly clear to all that it was Natalie's company and that she simply allowed him to work there. She was the creative force, the final say, and the engine behind the success of the company.

Nicole never stopped believing that it was fate that she and Nick met, but she also accepted the possibility that she and her daughter were the lucky recipients of a tragic misfortune — the death of Elizabeth.

In the evenings, when the sun's final rays passed through their bedroom window and touched Elizabeth's urn, it never failed to register with Nicole that it was Elizabeth who looked after her now. And as promised, Nick got into bed every night and whispered into Nicole's ear how much he loved her, and he held her tightly.

Acknowledgements

A big thank you to my lovely wife who has always been a pillar of support and love.

To beautiful Ava, profiles in courage come in all shapes, sizes and age groups.

To my great friend Frank Estrada. We have much in common, especially our love of Hemingway.

To my college roommate and close friend, Andres Lopez. Literature will always bond us.

A big thank you, to Lee Parpart for making *Per Verse Vengence* a much better book.

Another big thank you to Paula Chiarcos, my editor, for doing such an amazing and thoughtful job.

And to all the people at Iguana books, especially Meghan and Daniella, for being so patient and so very helpful.

CPSIA information can be obtained
at www.ICGtesting.com
Printed in the USA
LVHW020958191118
597622LV00007B/202/P

9 781771 802918